THERE'S SOMETHING HERE FROM SOMEWHERE ELSE

Jonathon T. Cross

That Spooky Beach LLC

Copyright © 2024 by Jonathon T. Cross

All rights reserved.

No part of this publication may be reproduced, distributed, or transmitted in any form or by any means, including photocopying, recording, or other electronic or mechanical methods, without the prior written permission of the publisher, except as permitted by U.S. copyright law. For permission requests, contact thatspookybeach@gmail.com

The story, all names, characters, and incidents portrayed in this production are fictitious. No identification with actual persons (living or deceased), places, buildings, and products is intended or should be inferred.

ISBN: 979-8-9883520-2-0

First edition 2024

Louisiana

Circa 1950

Lydia swung her arm back and with a flick of her wrist, she launched a smooth stone at the surface of the swamp. The murky waters swallowed her stone as soon as it hit, sending a spew of duckweed into the air. She pressed her eyes shut and inhaled a plentiful helping of muggy June air, wishing she could disappear before one of the local kids opened their mouths.

"Nice throw, gator breath." Maggie Dupont's voice carried over the splashes and croaks.

Lydia kicked her foot into the mud. "I meant to do that."

The truth was, Lydia could not skip stones, and she was not meant for the outdoors. She was a city girl, as the locals loved to point out. To her, everything in this town felt damp, muddy, and itchy. If it were up to her, she would never have left the hustle and bustle of city life.

The beautiful home she once knew had been replaced with a run-down swamp house in the most secluded backwater town she could imagine, and her new playground was an endless expanse of wetlands. Hostile creatures stalked her every move, including Maggie Dupont and her crew.

The swamp bubbled where Lydia's stone had hit, enticing Maggie to taunt, "It's almost dark, you know what that means." The other kids oohed, gossiping excitedly under their breath while Maggie put her arms up and staggered after Lydia. "The Lurker is going to get youuuu."

"Stop it!" Lydia said as she swatted at the mosquitoes flocking to her flushed cheeks.

"Quit hittin' yourself," Maggie said, recruiting the other kids to join in. "Quit hittin' yourself!"

The mosquitoes' spear-like mouths continued to pierce Lydia's skin, but she kept her hands locked to her sides while Maggie snickered. Lydia's body did not react well to mosquito bites. The tiny, pesky insects left her with inflamed, red welts that Maggie and her gang found hilarious. Lydia's throat tightened as tears welled in her eyes. Her fists were clenched. But rather than fight, she turned and fled.

As Lydia ran, a tree root caught her foot, sending her face first into the mud. Laughter filled the air as she picked herself off the ground, and it chased her all the way home, echoing off the foreboding cypress trees. She ran through a maze of foliage, ducking under Spanish moss and low-hanging branches, which snagged and pulled at her clothes until, at last, her parent's dilapidated stilt house came into view.

If only her parents understood what moving had done to her. There was not one good thing that came of it. She was ready to give them a piece of her mind, but when she neared the door to the decaying house, something remarkable lifted her spirits.

Sitting upright on top of the cracked wooden planks was the most beautiful doll Lydia had ever seen. She bent down and picked it up, noticing immediately how its bright blue eyes seemed to gaze right back into hers and how its curly blonde hair was as delicate as her own.

When she held the doll, an inexplicable feeling washed over her. It was as if this doll understood how she felt and promised to fill the void left in her heart. The doll's head was hard, made of something fragile like porcelain, but entirely unique, giving the doll's face a delicate, almost ethereal appearance, and the rosy blush on its cheeks only added to its charm. Its cushioned body was adorned with a blue and white checkered dress, like the one Lydia was wearing. She hugged her new doll, savoring the magical feeling of its soft fabric against her cheek as she ran inside.

Her mother, Helen, looked up from her knitting. "What on earth is that?"

"Sorry, I'll clean the mud up." Lydia squeezed her doll tighter. "And I love her. Thank you!"

Her father choked on his cigar smoke. "Don't hug it."

"My dolly?"

Helen wrinkled her nose, and turning to Lydia's father, asked, "Where did that doll come from, Richard?" Then, without waiting for an answer, she concluded. "It's probably diseased. Throw it away."

"But," Lydia stammered.

"No excuses," Helen said. "It's strange, and you're too old for dolls."

Lydia gazed at her doll; it was brand new. Not a single blemish or tear. "If you didn't buy her, then someone else got her for me."

Helen rolled her eyes. "Who would get *you* a doll?"

"Swamp people," Richard coughed through a thick cloud of smoke. "Always up to something."

"Can't I keep her?" Lydia asked, her fingers tightening around the doll.

"Absolutely not." Richard's tone grew accusatory. "I didn't move here so you could go gallivanting around town, drawing unwanted attention from these savages."

Lydia stomped her foot onto the floorboards. "I never wanted to move here at all."

"Lydia Kent," Helen's voice was sharp, cutting

through Lydia's defenses. "That's enough!"

With a quick motion, Helen pointed her finger at the doll, then to the door while signaling Richard with her eyes. Richard nodded, the cherry of his cigar glowing red as he set it down in the ashtray and peeled his body from his armchair.

Lydia looked up at him, feeling tiny in comparison as he held his hand out, expecting her to surrender her doll. He looked as menacing now as he had when he dragged her to the train station to move to this awful town. She still could not understand why he dragged them to the swamplands he seemed to hate so, but she was stuck, without toys, games, or people she could talk to, and feeling more like a piece of luggage than a child. There was no way she could let him take her new friend, too.

Her small fingers gripped the doll tightly when her father tried to take it, and his frustration only mounted when she refused to let go. With a grunt, Richard yanked the doll by its fragile head, and when Lydia fought back, he grabbed her by the wrist and suspended her in the air. Lydia winced, feeling the sting as her father delivered a vicious spanking. When the doll slipped from her hand, Richard dropped her. The pain was nothing, however, compared to the hurt she felt when she watched him march out the front door and toss her doll into the mud.

***

Lydia tossed and turned in bed that night, unable to fall asleep. Her cramped room was barely big enough for her twin-sized mattress, which was wedged up against a low-set windowsill. As she peered through the dusty, cobweb-covered panes, she saw the silhouette of her doll sprawled out on the ground in the moonlight. Her doll reflected the moon's pale glow, and its eyes sparkled with the intermittent green and yellow flash of the fireflies above; it was a faint but pretty radiance which spoke to the doll's beauty.

Lydia took a deep breath. As she exhaled, a flash of lightning illuminated the sky, followed by a deafening clap of thunder, which rattled the rickety old house. Droplets of heavy rain followed, as if the lightning had torn a hole in the sky. The fireflies went dark, and the water rose rapidly.

Tears fell from Lydia's eyes as she watched her doll being consumed by the muddy waters. Before long, it would be gone. Washed away to an unknown location, likely coming to rest in the belly of a gator or in the hands of some undeserving bully like Maggie Dupont.

The mere thought of Maggie's grubby hands on

her doll was enough to make Lydia's skin crawl. She let out a few trembling pants, trying to remain silent so her parents would not hear her cry. They did not like to be disturbed, which made what happened next even more terrifying. The front door rattled, not from the thunder, but from the forceful knock of a visitor.

Her father's footsteps echoed across the floorboards as he grumbled about "swamp people," among other needless insults. As Richard angrily answered the door, Lydia peeked out from her bedroom door to glimpse their visitor, a frail old woman.

The woman was standing on their porch, soaked by the rain and hunched over from exhaustion, panting as if she had run a mile. The cypress wood cane in her hand seemed to be her only lifeline as she struggled to remain upright. Despite her age, the woman had an enchanting sense of style that captivated Lydia.

Shells adorned the woman's headscarf, clinking as she swayed, and her arms jingled with each gesture as her bracelets and charms shifted. Large, patterned jewelry hung from her ears, adding to the eclectic collection of jewels and necklaces hanging from her neck. The woman introduced herself as Mama LeFleur, with a strained voice that crackled like a dying fire.

"I don't care who you are," Richard said. "Nobody comes knocking on my door at this hour."

Mama LeFleur cocked her head. "You've been here before."

"I'm afraid you're mistaken."

"I don't make mistakes." Mama LeFleur took a labored breath. "I sense great pain here," she said as she lifted her arm and pointed a slender finger at Lydia. "You."

Richard turned, glaring at Lydia. "Get back to bed and stay there."

Lydia slammed her bedroom door, then lay down to peer out from underneath it.

"I know you can hear me, child," Mama LeFleur said. "I feel your pain. Like a dark cloud hovering over your spirit. It's not right for a little girl to carry such heavy burdens. Come with me, and I'll heal the wounds in your spirit."

With that remark, Helen marched out to join the fight. "Who do you think you are?" she asked, then she turned to Richard and added, "Get this old bat out of my house."

Richard slammed the door on the woman, then quickly barricaded it with a chair he took from the dinner table. Lydia's heart pounded as his footsteps turned in her direction. She picked herself off the floor and sought refuge under the covers of her bed. When her father threw the bedroom door open, she held her breath, but he peered into the room for only a moment before slamming the door shut.

Lydia pulled the covers just below her eyes and looked out of the window to see if she could catch sight of the woman leaving, but she saw nothing. When she looked back at the spot where the doll had been, it was no longer there, which filled her heart with sorrow.

The rain had transformed the muddy ground into a shallow river, which flowed farther than her eyes could see. Part of her yearned to escape with the strange woman, Mama LeFleur. To follow the river and find her special doll and feel genuine compassion for more than just a fleeting moment. Lydia *was* in pain, and somehow Mama LeFleur knew that. Mama LeFleur knew it with such conviction that she braved the weather just to offer support.

The Search

Lydia set out early the next morning before the sun, or her parents, had risen. She was determined to retrieve her lost doll. The rain had stopped, and although the ground was still wet and spongy, the waters had receded. As she trotted alongside the lush vegetation lining the bank, she could feel the pull of thick mud weighing down her steps.

With any luck, her doll might have had a similar struggle, becoming stuck in the mire or entangled among the reeds before traveling too far. That hope fueled Lydia's search, but the more distance she covered, the more her optimism waned, replaced by a sense of hopeless desperation. Succumbing to the mud, her steps became sluggish, and her shoulders drooped as she trudged along.

She fell to her knees and dug through piles of foliage and felled branches. When digging failed, she diligently searched around the perimeter of the houses she passed. Depending on the houses' construction, she would crawl underneath their stilts to scour every inch of ground, while trying not to draw attention from the residents.

Before long, a thick layer of mud had clung to Lydia, bonding reeds and leaves to her clothes. She looked like a battered scarecrow who had wandered too far from its field, but there was one more house in sight, and she was determined to search it before giving up. The house looked abandoned, but just in case someone was home, she slid underneath it as quietly as she could. She could not, however, account for the sounds nature would make.

A terrible gurgle emanated from the swamp behind the home. She kept her head low, peering out beyond the stilts to get a view of the swamp. There was a gelatinous green film on the swamp's surface, which rose from the water like toxic bubble gum before popping in an explosion of duckweed. Smaller bubbles continued to rise around the central disturbance, concealing whatever lurked beneath.

Sometimes Lydia felt confident in her surroundings, as strange as they may be, but any semblance of control she felt was stolen when the ground beneath her trembled with the same terror she felt welling inside. She knew there were gators in the swamp, but the drone rising from the bubbling disturbance was unlike anything she could imagine. The sound seemed to reach inside her mind, creating sporadic and overwhelming thoughts.

Without taking her eyes off the commotion, Lydia used her arms to push herself backwards. She pushed until she had slid herself clear out from under the house. Her eyes were still locked on the swamp when an unidentifiable mass breached its surface, and just as it did, she felt her heel collide with a solid object behind her. Lydia jumped to her feet, turning to face the obstruction.

A puzzled young boy met her stare. "Something wrong with you?" he asked.

"The swamp." Lydia directed the boy's attention to the gurgling pit, but the water had stilled. "I swear it was just...I just..." She took a few steps closer to the water, but the boy grabbed her arm.

"You shouldn't have come here," he said.

Lydia pulled her arm away. "Excuse me? I'm telling you I saw something."

"Nothing worth seeing here."

Lydia was taken aback by the boy's attitude. He spoke with the condemnation of an adult, though he was just a boy about her age. She balled her fists, ready to speak her mind, but as she looked into his chestnut brown eyes, her grip softened. Compared to the other boys around town, he appeared stronger, more capable, yet somewhat sweet beneath it all.

His presence brought a sense of calm to her thoughts and slowed her breathing. It was only recently that Lydia had decided boys could be cute, and she typically did not gawk, but she could not help admiring the way his smooth, light brown skin glistened under the rising sun. The boy was clutching a fishing stick in his right hand and a steel tackle box in his left, the weight of which made his arm flex, and for a moment, Lydia forgot about the swamp, and her doll.

"Do you live here?" she asked. "I didn't mean to upset you. It's just that I lost my doll, and I've been looking for her everywhere."

The boy exhaled heavily through his nose. "Course I don't live here," he said. "Neither do you. Why would your doll be here?"

Lydia wiped the mud from her face and arms, hoping to look less disastrous as she justified her actions to the boy, noting how the rain had carried her doll away the night before. When recounting the details, she felt a lump form in her throat, and she had to take a deep breath to keep from crying. As she continued, she could sense a change in the boy's demeanor; his expression softened. Unlike the other locals she had met since moving, he took the time to listen to what she had to say. After she explained her situation, he told her not to worry about it because his dad was the sheriff.

"I'm not allowed visitors," he said. "But Pa might make an exception since it's for a case."

There was a moment of hesitation while Lydia weighed her options. Her father always warned her to avoid authority figures and never to answer their questions, but the boy's dad sounded okay. Not like the police from the big city where she was from.

Those police had come to her parents' house uninvited and demanded to speak with them as soon as she opened the door. They were gruff and sent her to her room because she "shouldn't be around when grownups were talking." There was plenty of shouting after that, and it kept on until her parents chased him away.

The boy waved his fishing stick, breaking Lydia from her memories. "My name's Jaxson. Jaxson Hayes. Follow me." Jaxson flicked his head to the side, then took off in that direction.

"I'm Lydia," she said as she hurried after him.

Although the town was a swampy, hostile cesspool, she felt better when she walked alongside Jaxson. He was like a safety net, catching the stress and anxiety before it reached her. She was not worried about the gators or the snakes slithering nearby, nor did she dwell on what she had seen in the swamp. Perhaps her distress over the doll had gotten the better of her, she reasoned, and as Jaxson led her fearlessly through the marsh, she was just excited to learn more about him.

To Lydia's delight, Jaxson was an open book, and he talked without taking a breath. It was as if he had not spoken to another person in years, and she loved every second. During their brief journey to his home, she learned more about him than she ever did about her old city friends. Jaxson was born in the town, and his father had grown up locally too. Sadly, Jaxson's mother left town when he was just five years old and never came back, which is when his dad, the sheriff, became his sole caretaker. But what Jaxson said next was of grave concern.

"The Lurker cursed my pa."

Lydia shuddered, remembering Maggie taunting her about the Lurker. It was a creature the kids used to tease each other with. "There's no such thing, right?"

"Never seen it, but I'm darn sure it's here. No one much talks to me. Town's pretty much turned on my pa too." Jaxson closed his eyes and exhaled. "Not their fault. They just don't want to be cursed."

"I don't believe in curses."

"How else would you explain my ma leaving?" Jaxson asked. "And my pa. He hasn't felt right since he was little. He said there's evil here. That's why he made himself the sheriff, to protect people from it."

"You can't make yourself a sheriff."

"Sure can," Jaxson said as he directed her gaze towards a wooded area.

At first glance, the thicket appeared commonplace, but as they drew closer, shapes took form. There was a cozy-looking cottage nestled behind a giant oak tree and draped in Spanish moss. It was as if Jaxson's dad had deliberately camouflaged their home to blend in with the surrounding flora, a desperate man's attempt to discourage others from seeking him out.

Jaxson dropped his tackle box on the porch and leaned his fishing stick against the wall, then he wiped his feet on the coarse welcome mat and opened the door. "I brought company," he announced as he waved Lydia inside.

"Company?" Sheriff Hayes rose from his seat with urgency, his hand pressed against his lower back. His face, lined with age and experience, wore a solemn expression, and his voice, although strong, carried a hint of sorrow beneath its thick Cajun accent. "Never seen you around here before."

"I just moved to town."

"That's unfortunate," the Sheriff huffed.

"Lydia lost her doll in the storm," Jaxson said, attempting to sway the conversation. "Someone might have taken it from outside her place. Sounded like a job for the sheriff."

"Oh no," Sheriff Hayes grunted. "I'm not looking

for no doll."

Jaxson glared at his father. "Why not?"

Sheriff Hayes gave Lydia a dubious glare. "Well alright, go on then."

Lydia ignored the discomfort of the Sheriff's presence and meticulously described the doll, hoping he would help her find it. From the unique material comprising its fragile head to its soft, stuffed feet, no detail went unnoted.

Sheriff Hayes' expression was hard to read as she recounted the details. He leaned close to listen, investigating her every word. She told him about the doll's bright blue eyes, which seemed to stare right back at her. And the bow the doll wore on its head, which looked identical to her own, and the charming blue and white dress which flowed delicately over its body.

"No one can ever claim it's theirs," Lydia said, leaning in. "She looks just like me."

The Sheriff's face fell, and he shuddered as his skin contracted into goosebumps. For a moment, he appeared to be frozen. Then, without warning, he grabbed Lydia's shoulders, turned her around, and hurried her out the front door. Jaxson ran after them, shouting for his dad to stop, but the Sheriff ordered him back inside. Once Jaxson was out of sight, the Sheriff knelt next to Lydia and placed a hand on her shoulder.

"You don't belong here," he said, his voice cutting through Lydia's heart like a knife. "I'm sorry. You're a sweet girl, but I cannot risk nothing happening to my boy. You stay away from us."

There's Something Wrong

Dusk crept up fast, and Lydia was nearly out of strength when she spotted her parents' house. Without Jaxson guiding her back, the repeating pattern of vegetation and trees had become a blur. Soon, the faint light of the fireflies was her only welcome company.

The swampland's noises had grown louder when the sun retired, enveloping her in a horrific symphony of hisses and wails. Reeds rustled, offset by unseen footsteps, and the howling wind chased her through the marsh. Never had she been so thankful as when she saw her parents' dilapidated house in the distance, even though she knew exactly what awaited her when she opened the door. It was the same thing she always returned to. Disappointment.

Sure enough, the moment she stepped through the front door, her parents' scorn was there to greet her. Her father mumbled swears about her wandering around town. Not out of concern as a loving parent would, but out of contempt for her ability to attract the attention of the "swamp people."

Neither her father nor mother cared to ask how her day was, where she had been, or why she had returned home panting and covered from head to toe in dried mud. So, she took it upon herself to offer justification, recounting her visit to Jaxson's cottage, and subsequent confusion over the Sheriff's attitude.

"Wasn't bad enough you brought the old woman here?" Richard stamped his cigar out and slapped Lydia across the face. "You've made nice with a lawman. Of all the things you could have done."

"I was looking for my doll."

Helen left her knitting on the couch and grabbed Lydia's arm. "Don't talk back to your father."

Lydia spotted an empty glass bottle on the counter and knew she was at the mercy of her parents. They never listened when they drank from the glass bottle. Sometimes one of her parents would be in a mood, while the other would be decent, but when they joined forces, her best move was to keep quiet and obey. Right now, that meant letting her mother drag her to her room.

Once Lydia was in her room, her mother shut the door, and a moment later she heard her father's footsteps, followed by hammering, which echoed through the walls. It was not the first time he had boarded her door. He liked to make sure she could not cause him trouble.

Knowing that she would not be let out, even for dinner, Lydia collapsed onto her bed, and that was when she saw it. Her doll. It was lying there, with the covers pulled up to its chin, and its bright blue eyes fixed on her. Lydia peered at the doll, wondering how it had gotten there. She knew it could not have been her parents; they hated it.

The hair on her neck stood erect as she realized someone must have snuck into her room and placed the doll there. She gazed around the tight walls and peeked under the bed, but there was no trace of anyone. Whoever it was had spent a great deal of time and effort, though. The doll's blue and white checkered dress, which had become a mess in the storm, was as clean as it had been when she first saw it.

Perhaps Mama LeFleur picked the doll up on her way out and cleaned it. Lydia got under the covers and snuggled up to her doll's fresh linen, feeling a sense of relief and renewal to have a friend she could cuddle with as the shadows took hold. Swamp houses did not have electricity like her old house did, but the doll seemed to emit a faint, airy glow and provide the type of warmth only a human ought to.

"I'm going to call you Sophie," Lydia whispered. "You're going to be my friend."

She cradled the doll in her arms, feeling its warmth and softness, and poured her heart out to it. And despite the muggy heat surrounding her, Lydia could not help but shiver as a chill ran down her spine. She held the doll in front of her face, sure it had made a noise as it listened to her stories, and in studying its intricate eyes and perfectly painted lips, she wondered if there was something more to it. Something she could not quite put her finger on.

The farther she held the doll from her chest, the more her hands seemed to tremble in revolt. The doll's outstretched arms called out to her, and she could not resist the urge to hold her doll as close to her heart as possible. When Lydia squeezed the soft fabric body again, she felt whole, even as her parents bickered in the adjacent room about what to do.

Richard's voice carried the loudest. "We need to get rid of it."

"We're not staying, are we?" Helen asked, her voice barely penetrating the wall.

"There's nowhere else to go."

"Fine." Helen's tone grew shrill. "But why the real ones?"

There was a pause before Richard responded. "No one needs to know we're Kents."

Lydia folded her pillow over her ears, wondering what her parents were arguing over, and what was wrong with being a Kent. She had always known not to give strangers or authorities her last name, but she did not know why. At least for now, her parents were not getting rid of her. She turned to her side, trying to ignore the intrusive thoughts which consumed her mind, and instead watched the fireflies flicker outside her window. It worked for a time. Until the fireflies retreated and her parents marched outside.

Both her mother and father stood in the moonlight, shoveling a pit into the wet earth. Shortly after they finished digging, her father dumped a bag and some liquid into the pit, then lit a match and tossed it in.

Lydia shut her eyes as a fireball shot into the sky, and when she opened them, her parents were gone. She was not sure what they burned, only why. It was because she had talked to the Sheriff. They did not want him to know who they were, and they did not want anyone to know their surname.

A pit formed in Lydia's stomach, but in response to that distress, her doll emitted a deep, comforting glow. She marveled as warmth radiated from the doll's head, pulsing as it enveloped and eased her troubled spirit. There was an undeniable sense of magic about her doll, and in its embrace, she fell into a heavy slumber.

***

Lydia rose to the scent of burning wood and the distinctive crackle of fire. As she peered through the smoke, she could see flames flickering between the fractured walls. She held her shirt up to her mouth and hurried to the door, but when she tried to push it open, she found her parents had left it blocked. She screamed, trying to raise her voice above the sound of the roaring flames, but no one came.

Heat blistered her hands as she pounded on the door. When her efforts failed, she jumped onto her bed and tried to force the window open, but no matter how hard she pushed and pulled at it, the old frame would not budge. She knocked out several panes, gasping for air, but she could not break through the grid, so she dropped onto her mattress and squeezed the doll tight, hoping she had not imagined its magic.

When all hope seemed lost, the doll's eyes sparkled, and its glassy face emitted a glow stronger than before. This was no trick of the moonlight, nor the stolen radiance of a firefly. This glow came directly from her doll, and it spread through Lydia, making her feel as though she and the doll shared one spirit. Her eyes remained transfixed on the doll as her door fell from its hinges, and a wall of flame burst through the opening.

"Help!" Lydia screamed as her bed was engulfed in a chaotic dance of bright yellow and orange.

Somewhere New

Lydia sat motionless on her bed, clutching her doll tightly to her chest. Her eyes were as still as her body, unable to comprehend what they had witnessed. When dawn broke, it cast new light on the rubble which lay around her, ushering in a breeze that helped to clear the smoke from the smoldering embers. Although the edge of her bed had caught fire, it was quickly extinguished by the doll's light, which served as a protective bubble.

Neither flame nor smoke permeated the bubble, leaving Lydia to sit and watch as the fire burned her room to the ground. When the wall separating their rooms fell, Lydia watched her parents' bodies fall prey to the heat, bubbling and charring like hot dogs roasted over a campfire. Her parents never rose to the chaos, subdued by the glass bottle finished between them. Hours later, most of the wooden structure collapsed, and Lydia's bed fell onto the muddy earth below, in a pile of ash and burning embers.

"Don't look at their bodies, child." Mama LeFleur hobbled through the scene using her cane to sweep aside charred bits of wood, and stepping carefully through the mud, she arrived at Lydia's side. "I knew something like this was coming. I could feel it in my bones." She paused for a moment, deep in thought. "Ricky was always trouble."

Startled out of her trance, Lydia's eyes met Mama LeFleur's. "My dad?"

"Come on now, child. Let's get you cleaned up."

Lydia hesitated, unsure of what to do. "I'm not allowed to go with strangers."

"I'm afraid you have no choice," Mama LeFleur said firmly. "Ain't no one here to stop you, neither. Now come along before that old Sheriff pokes his nose around. No telling where he'd send you."

Lydia's eyes lingered on the smoldering remains of her parents, the scent of death filling her nostrils as Mama LeFleur dragged her away from the scene. Despite all the pain her mother and father had caused, Lydia could not deny the love she felt for them. Love, which turned to sorrow as their ashes whipped through the air, taunting her, while the persistent sound of crackling flames still rang within her ears.

Confusion set in, then fear took hold. She squeezed her doll's hand, dragging it through the marsh behind her. Maybe Jaxson's curse *was* real, and she had it. Maybe there was something wrong with her parents. Regardless of anything, her doll had saved her. Whoever created it was no mere doll maker. They had imbued her doll with a spirit all its own, gifting it with passion, love, and the power to save lives.

***

Lydia froze at the sight of Mama LeFleur's swamp house, which was more like a swamp mansion. Vines crept across the exterior wood panels. Although warped and showing its age, the paneling still held an air of magnificence. The steep slant of the roof cast an enormous shadow, which blotted out the sun, and beneath it on the porch, decayed wooden chairs rocked back and forth in the wind as if occupied by unseen visitors. It was equal parts haunting and beautiful. Mama LeFleur told her that the home was rich in spirit and history, and as soon as Lydia stepped inside, she knew the old woman's words were true.

Faint light seeped in through the moss-covered windows, casting a soft glow on the smoke-filled room. The air circulating inside Mama LeFleur's house was rich with the scent of incense and herbs, which combined to create a unique and intoxicating aroma all their own.

Lydia ran her hands over the intricately woven rugs which adorned the walls, and somehow lost sight of the tragedy which had just occurred, and the pain associated with it. Becoming entranced by the talismans, amulets, and charms which hung from the walls between the rugs and glass jars filled with herbs, roots, and dried flowers sat atop makeshift driftwood shelves. In the center of the grand room was a large round table, cluttered with stones, shells, feathers, and bones.

As Lydia took a seat at the table, she felt a sense of calm wash over her, as if time itself had slowed to allow her to savor the moment. Comfort, although fleeting, found her as she blocked the memory of the fire from her mind and sipped on a cup of tea that Mama LeFleur provided.

Things were still until Mama sensed an interruption was imminent and set her teacup down on the table. Sure enough, a knock at the door shattered their peaceful refuge, causing Mama to shake her head and mutter something to herself. Lydia turned her attention to the door, wishing their visitor would disappear so she could return to the moment of peace and freedom she was feeling.

Mama LeFleur, however, hobbled to the door, her cane clicking against the wooden floorboards until she reached it. "I knew you'd come poking your nose around here," she said as she opened the door.

Sheriff Hayes peered past Mama LeFleur. "Ain't surprised to see the girl," he said. "There was a fire down the way. Burned passports and IDs, and a couple of unidentified—"

Mama shushed the sheriff. "Her parents."

"Thing is, there wasn't any wind last night." The Sheriff shifted his gait. "Can't imagine how a pitted fire spread to a damp house and didn't touch nothing else."

"You got a point, Elijah?"

"The girl's got a doll." Sheriff Hayes' voice grew firm. "You know as well as I do what that means, and your parlor tricks ain't going to protect her. I'll take her where she needs to go."

"I don't want to leave," Lydia said, hiding behind Mama LeFleur with her doll held close.

Sheriff Hayes beckoned with a flick of his fingers. "It's best for everyone that you do."

Mama LeFleur's muscles tensed as she hardened her stance. "I'll adopt her."

"She's an outsider." The Sheriff shook his head. "There's only one suitable place for an outsider."

"Call yourself a sheriff all you want, Elijah. Doesn't make it so. You ain't got no power here, and you can't take her against her will." Mama LeFleur knelt and placed her hands on Lydia's shoulders. "Tell me, child, what would you like to do?"

Lydia shifted her weight from one foot to the other, her toe digging into the creaky floorboards. She found Sheriff Hayes to be terrifying, and the idea of spending time with him was no more appealing than the idea of him sending her away. Mama LeFleur may be a stranger, but Lydia felt safe in Mama's care, and she felt loved within these walls.

"I want to stay," Lydia said.

Sheriff Hayes squinted at her. "I don't know where you came from, or what Mama LeFleur wants with you, but if you won't listen to reason, there ain't nothing I can do to help you."

Mama LeFleur slammed the door and let out a frustrated sigh. "Don't pay him no mind, child. He doesn't trust no one, particularly people like me. Poor man ain't been right since he was a kid."

Mama led Lydia back to the table and shared more about the sheriff and his distaste for the clairvoyant, or anyone in communion with the world beyond our own, which Mama LeFleur claimed to be. She used the phrase "half of a man" to describe Sheriff Hayes, clarifying that she did not mean it as an insult and that it was not his fault.

The sheriff was born a twin, and when twins are born, she explained, each sibling shares a soul, which is divided between their two bodies. For that reason,

Sheriff Hayes and his twin sister were inseparable, like two sides of the same coin. What one sibling experienced, so did the other, and that was just fine when they were kids, until the world ripped them apart. It was then that Mama LeFleur's story took a dark turn, and Lydia found herself unable to shake the feeling of unease that settled in her chest.

Years ago, when Sheriff Hayes' parents moved him and his twin sister Jean to town, Jean received a doll much like the one that arrived on Lydia's stoop, except that it looked just like Jean did. As the town succumbed to fires, animal attacks, and brutal murders, the doll protected Jean and, by extension, Elijah. Mama's details were hazy, but she said the tragedies culminated in a hurricane, which brought the town to its knees and swept Jean away, leaving Elijah without his other half.

"Why didn't Jean's doll protect her?" Lydia asked.

"That's the same question little Elijah asked." Mama LeFleur shook her head. "Dolls can only do so much, child. There's something here, you see: From somewhere else. A Lurker, in the marsh."

Lydia nodded, her fingers trembling around her cup of tea, as she tried to process Mama's words. "And Elijah's not a real sheriff?"

"Just a man with strong opinions, child."

"My parents were scared for nothing..." Lydia

brought the teacup to her lips.

Mama LeFleur grabbed Lydia's wrist before she could take another sip. "Leave a little tea at the bottom," she said. "Then hold your cup strong and give it three good swirls."

Lydia followed Mama's instructions and gave her teacup three strong swirls, causing the liquid to slosh around inside. Then she flipped the cup on Mama's command, letting the rest of her tea spill out onto the floor.

Mama LeFleur took the cup and inspected it, tilting it to get a better view of the tea leaves stuck to the inside. Her wrinkled face contorted as she gazed pensively at the designs and patterns in the cup. To Lydia, the leaves looked like a random assortment of specks and dots, but to Mama, they were significant.

Grouped together, the leaf fragments formed symbols which revealed a story of Lydia's past, present, and future. Mama read the tea leaves with intense concentration, punctuated only by the occasional "mmm" and "hm." The anticipation of what the leaves would say about her future made Lydia's palms sweat and her heart beat faster.

With a mournful expression, Mama set the teacup down and turned her gaze to Lydia. "There's a storm coming, child."

Lydia looked up at Mama LeFleur, confronted

with a sad truth that had plagued her everywhere she went for as long as she could remember. "I don't belong here."

"You belong with me, child." Mama LeFleur wiped away Lydia's tears. "I know life feels scary right now, but I think you're just what this town needs."

"Really?"

Mama nodded. "When the storm passes, we'll all be whole, and you'll have yourself a new home."

Lydia trusted Mama, but not Elijah. "Where did the Sheriff want to send me?"

"Somewhere you shouldn't go." Mama looked uncomfortable as she answered, "There's a woman who lives in the woods outside of town. She's, well...something ain't right with her head. Never has been."

The Lurker

With time's passage, Lydia felt the sharp edges of her pain soften and blur, becoming absorbed by her doll or diluted by the soothing warmth of one of Mama LeFleur's many herbal concoctions. Lydia found a sense of tranquility at Mama's. The fire was always burning steadily, and the teakettle screamed like clockwork throughout the day. It was as if Mama had a never-ending supply of teas, perfectly matched to every situation, thought, and feeling which one could encounter, always on hand and ready to serve at a moment's notice.

It did not take long for curiosity to overcome Lydia's sorrow, but her fear persisted. "Tell me about the Lurker," she said as she glanced over at Mama.

"It's no concern of yours, child." Mama took a seat next to Lydia at the table, a warm smile spread across her face. "You should be outside making friends. Not stuck in here with me."

Within the confines of Mama's house, Lydia felt a

sense of security, but she could not escape her lingering fear of the unknown dangers waiting just beyond its walls. "The Lurker is out there."

"Always has been." Mama placed her hand on Lydia's cheek, offering comfort and reassurance. "Doesn't mean you need to stop living your life. You got that doll of yours for a reason. Now, finish up your tea, go outside, and be a child. Leave the worrying to me."

Without uttering a word, Lydia communicated her thoughts to Mama through her eyes.

"It'll be okay," Mama said, her voice calm and confident as she handed Lydia her doll. "Keep this close to your heart and stay clear of the still waters."

Even in the mildest of disagreements, Mama's unwavering resolve made it impossible for Lydia to win. The past few weeks in Mama's house taught her that Mama had a way of getting what she wanted, whether it was through gentle persuasion or relentless determination.

Despite her initial resistance, Lydia eventually embraced her new sundown bedtime, and she now savored each meal's abundant servings of vegetables with no complaints. So, when Mama stood from the table and opened the front door, Lydia knew she could not refrain from walking through it.

The air wafting in from outside was smokeless,

carrying the distant and now unfamiliar scent of nature. Lydia's heart raced at the mere thought of what lay ahead. She stood from the table and held her doll against her chest, taking a deep breath before gathering her courage and walking through the door. As she stood on the porch, the buzzing insects and calling birds that had seemed so muted from inside Mama's house once again enveloped her in their vibrant sounds.

Mama LeFleur smiled. "You feel that child. Takes a pinch of sunshine to get your mind off things."

Lydia looked back at Mama, her lips curling into a forced smile. Although she felt more confident venturing back into town, Lydia could not bring herself to tell Mama that none of the kids liked her. There were no potential friends to make, and the one friend she had made was forbidden from seeing her.

No, her time would not be wasted on play, but she could engage in other activities, like figuring out what the Lurker wanted from her. Mama remained tight-lipped about the creature, but the townsfolk might be more forthcoming with information. If Lydia wanted to survive as an outsider, then she needed to immerse herself in the sights and sounds of the town, understand what challenges she would face, and most importantly, familiarize herself with the creature that lurked in these still waters.

***

The Lurker proved to be as divisive as it was pervasive. Lydia interviewed many of the town's residents, half of whom vehemently denied the existence of the Lurker. They claimed that the myth was born out of a hostile environment and a history of accident-prone newcomers like herself.

When Lydia pointed to her doll as proof of a supernatural resistance, she was met with their mocking laughter. The rest of the people she interviewed had much stronger reactions. Mere mention of the cryptid caused them to become on edge, their eyes darting around anxiously as they spoke to her in hushed tones, either avoiding the topic of her doll or studying it cautiously. The believers were older than their skeptical counterparts, but they shooed her away all the same, offering little meaningful guidance. As sundown approached, Lydia advanced to the last house with weary steps.

A woman opened the door before Lydia could knock. "We don't want you here."

Lydia wedged her foot between the door and its frame, preventing the woman from shutting it. "Please, I need to know about the Lurker."

The woman scoffed, the sound of her disdain echoing through the stale air as she retreated inside. However, she left the door ajar, allowing Lydia to slip in behind her. As Lydia stepped into the home, her eyes landed on a family portrait displayed on the fireplace mantel.

In the photograph, a young child stood next to the woman, their hazy eyes filled with tender innocence. Lydia immediately recognized the girl as Maggie Dupont, who, despite her youthful and pleasant appearance in the photograph, had grown into quite a miserable bully.

"Mrs. Dupont," Lydia said, directing her gaze back to the woman.

Mrs. Dupont picked the meaning straight out of Lydia's tone. "Maggie's not so bad, you know." She said, taking a seat in her worn armchair. "She's been taught to avoid outsiders like yourself. The Lurker maintains harmony with its community, but now and then, someone new comes and causes a stir."

"If you're worried about Maggie, why don't you go somewhere else?"

"The Lurker needs us..." Mrs. Dupont sank deeper into the ripped cushion of her armchair, releasing a heavy sigh. "And we need it."

Lydia cocked her head, puzzled by Mrs. Dupont's cryptic remark.

"Our bodies and minds become entangled with the Lurker," Mrs. Dupont explained. "And when people leave town, something breaks inside them. They go bad. Most are compelled back and punished."

Lydia recalled Mama and the Sheriff talking about a woman who lived in the forest outside of town. "The woman in the woods," Lydia said. "Did she go bad?"

"She went something," Mrs. Dupont replied. "She and her brother Ricky used to live down the way when we were kids."

"Ricky?" Lydia froze, a vivid memory of Mama calling her father "Ricky" flooding her mind.

"That's right."

"What was his sister's name?"

"No one's used her real name in so long I've forgotten it, but when Sheriff Elijah and his sister moved to town, we all used to play together." Mrs. Dupont paused and shook her head. "Well, if you're asking, then you must know. After Elijah's sister disappeared, Ricky's sister lost it. She ran away from her family, into the woods and never came back. Her parents took her for dead and moved away with Ricky."

If Lydia's inclination was correct, her father was Ricky, and he had lived in this town as a child. That would explain his compulsion to return and the resulting punishment which befell him. He was always gruff, rugged, and abrasive, but at times, he showed glimpses of his human side. It was as if a dark cloud hung over his thoughts, preventing him from fully loving her or protecting her like a father should.

Believing such callous behavior was not his fault appealed to Lydia, offering a glimmer of comfort in the void left by the loss of both her parents. But this revelation meant something more. The woman in the woods might be a blood relative, whose resilience prevented the Lurker from gaining control over her all these years. Maybe deep down, Lydia harbored the same hidden potential within herself.

"I need to find the woman," Lydia said, feeling hopeful about her situation.

Mrs. Dupont shook her head. "The suns falling, doll. You'd best get yourself home before it sets."

Maggie Dupont

The next morning, Lydia set off to find Jaxson, hoping he could guide her to the mysterious woman in the woods. She left Mama's house without making a sound, mindful of the fact that Mama had been asleep when she returned the night before and was still fast asleep now.

The thought of Mama's response to her breaking curfew filled her with anxiety. If disobeying Mama was anything like disobeying her parents, she was in for a lashing and a grounding. Lydia shuddered, imagining the whipcrack of her father's belt and the lingering scent of aged leather, but swiftly wiped the memory from her mind. A lashing she could handle, a grounding she could not abide. She needed to delve into her family's history, understand her relationship to the woman living in the woods, and learn how the Lurker tied into it all.

Lydia eventually spotted Jaxson standing by the water's edge, his back turned towards her. She called out to him, but his gaze remained fixed on the still water. When she called out again, he turned his head to meet her, remaining silent. She hurried towards him, but as soon as she got near, he turned and headed the other way. With mounting frustration, Lydia quickened her pace, and as she did, Jaxson broke into a sprint, forcing her to chase him through the marsh. Feeling both embarrassed and resentful, Lydia raised her voice and demanded he stop and listen to her.

"I can't talk to you," Jaxson said as he leaned against the bark of a massive oak tree.

Lydia stomped her foot into the muddy ground. "Why not?"

"That's why." Jaxson pointed at the doll hanging from Lydia's hand. "I've got enough curse as it is, what with my family and all. Pa says your doll is bad luck. My aunt had one just like it."

"Did your dad tell you what happened?" Lydia took a labored breath. "To my parents."

Jaxson nodded, unsure what to say.

"You don't understand." Lydia held her doll up with conviction. "Sophie saved me from the fire."

"Dolls can't save no one."

Lydia tapped her foot. "If Sophie can't save no one, then she can't be bad luck either."

"Shhh." Jaxson raised a finger to his mouth, signaling for silence. They heard the rustling of reeds, followed by a shrill hiss that sent shivers down their spines and made Jaxson instinctively grasp Lydia's hand. "Best get out of here."

They hurried down the bank, adrenaline pumping through their veins, until a blood-curdling scream pierced the air behind them. Lydia's grip on her doll tightened, and she cried out, pivoting her body to face the source of the scream. That was when she spotted Maggie Dupont, her back pressed against the oak tree, gasping for breath between fits of laughter.

"Not funny." Lydia caught her breath, her heart pounding in her chest. "You scared me!"

"Scared the Lurker will get you," Maggie taunted. "Figures you two freaks would find each other."

"We're not freaks," Lydia said, and recalling her conversation with Mrs. Dupont, added, "You're the one who's scared of the Lurker. Guess that's why you're such a jerk!"

Jaxson tugged at Lydia's hand. "Come on, let's go."

Lydia conceded, allowing Jaxson to lead her away, but Maggie snuck up behind them and snatched the doll from Lydia's hand. Before Lydia could react, Maggie had tossed her doll into the swamp.

"You get Lydia's doll right now," Jaxson snapped, his patience wearing thin.

"Relax," Maggie said, as she walked to the water's

edge. "I'm messing around with her anyhow."

Maggie reached her hand into the thick, sludgy water and grabbed the doll, but her eyes bulged when something caught her arm. As her body thrashed from side to side, the water rippled and frothed around her. She let out a scream that sent chills down Lydia's spine, and her eyes filled with sheer terror as she looked back.

Jaxson ran and yanked Maggie out of the water. They lost their balance and tumbled backwards. Jaxson hit the ground first, followed by Maggie and Lydia's doll.

Maggie clutched her stomach, laughing even harder than before. "Too easy," she said, rising to her feet with her eyebrow cocked. "Now, who's afraid of the Lurk—"

Before she could finish, a gator surfaced and clamped down on her leg. She let out a panicked cry as her body hit the ground. Jaxson grabbed her hands and gave her a desperate tug. But the gator's grip was rock solid, and Maggie's body refused to budge. The gator clenched its jaws with increasing force.

Maggie's screams echoed through the swamp as her shinbone crunched under the pressure. Blood spurted from the fresh wound, filling the air with a metallic scent that made Lydia vomit. With a violent thrash of its head, the massive gator flung Maggie through the air and sent Jaxson hurtling into the murky depths of the swamp. Maggie was barely clinging to life, her body drenched in tears and blood, her fingers digging frantically into the mud.

Lydia abandoned her doll and lunged for Maggie, but the gator was too quick. It seized Maggie by the head this time, bringing her screams to a sudden stop before retreating beneath the water. Lydia's heart raced as she approached the swamp. The stillness was deafening. Then the gator thrashed violently with Maggie's head still in its grasp.

Several times it rolled, splashing Lydia with a mixture of swamp water and blood, and causing a series of sickening snaps, rips, and tears to seal themselves in her mind. On its last roll, the gator separated Maggie's head from her body and swallowed it whole, while another gator, attracted by the commotion, stole the lion's share of the kill.

Jaxson burst from the murky water; his sudden appearance shattered Lydia's state of shock. She snatched her doll off the ground and turned to run, but her ankle twisted in a patch of wet earth, sending her to the ground. Taking advantage of the opportunity, a gator lunged towards her. Lydia squeezed her eyelids shut and gripped her doll, preparing for the deadly bite.

Seconds passed, and then nothing. Feeling the gator's humid breath, she cautiously opened her eyes.

The massive gator stood perfectly immobile, mere inches from her face. Its gaping mouth and menacing teeth were fully exposed, yet it remained docile. Her doll's luminous glow was reflected in the gator's glassy eyes, subduing it with a force beyond her comprehension. The next thing she knew, Jaxson was dragging her away from the stunned reptile.

The Fog

Once they were safe from the gators, Jaxson released his grip on Lydia and collapsed, exhausted, on the ground beside her. Their eyes met, and she held his gaze in silence until the shadows grew long. What they had just witnessed left them at a loss for words and unsure of what would happen next.

Lydia remained still, with her mind stuck on the terrible memory of Maggie Dupont, recollecting the horrid rips, tears, and pops which brought bile to her throat. Her parents' post-mortem remains had been hard enough to look at, but watching the life leaving Maggie's eyes was something she could never un-see.

"Maggie was right there."

Jaxson put his hand on Lydia's shoulder. "We did everything we could."

Lydia nodded, allowing his touch to free her thoughts.

"It stopped glowing." Jaxson nodded at the doll in her hands, in awe, much like she had been when she first experienced the doll's magic. "Just now, but why?"

"The danger is gone," Lydia said. "And when you touched me, I felt better."

"Huh?"

"When I'm scared, or hurting, Sophie makes me feel better. She knows I'm okay now, and that you're here…"

"We need to tell my pa about Maggie."

Lydia sat up and pulled her doll in close. "No way. Your dad will blame Sophie. He'll try to take her away from me. Mama said there's a storm coming, and I need her to protect us."

Jaxson stood, conflict written on his face. "Maggie's been killed," he said. "My pa said that doll is no good. He needs to know what happened so he can tell us what to do next. He's the sheriff, and he always knows what's best."

Before Lydia could rise to her feet, she glimpsed Jaxson's determined expression as he bolted for his dad's cottage. She dug her feet into the muddy ground, shaking off the haze that clouded her mind, and chased after him, calling out for him to stop. He shouted back with conviction, urging her to believe in his father's judgment.

As Jaxson's lead grew, Lydia gave up on shouting at him, and when she did, she noticed her doll was humming. The sound sent shivers down her spine and brought her legs to an abrupt halt. Looking at the doll, she felt its unnerving glow, and she knew something awful was lurking in the woods. When she looked up again, Jaxson had disappeared without a trace. She turned, her eyes scanning the landscape, taking in every detail. Nothing looked familiar. In every direction stretched an identical and disorienting collection of thickets.

"Please help me," Lydia whispered to her doll, tears welling in her eyes.

A low rumble sounded from behind her, growing louder with each passing moment. She turned, her heart racing as she came face to face with a wolf. Its snout was inches away from her face, saliva dripping from its long, sharp canines. The beast's hot breath lingered in the air, carrying the distinct scent of meat. Never had she encountered an animal with such sharp, pointy ears and penetrating eyes. The wolf's tail stood erect, with its nostrils flared, catching the scent of its prey.

Lydia held her breath as the wolf investigated her doll, its nose twitching with anticipation. The wolf's eyes were fixed on the doll, and its growling grew louder and more intense until it erupted into a series of disgruntled barks. Lydia's grip on the doll tightened, provoking the wolf's anger. Its snout wrinkled as it closed in, nipping at her hands. In response, her doll emitted a powerful, blinding light that grew stronger, causing the wolf to yelp loudly.

Emerging from the thicket, Jaxson hurled a rock, striking the wolf's head. "Get out of here!"

With a burst of aggression, the wolf ripped Lydia's doll from her hands, leaving her vulnerable as it darted away.

"I knew you wouldn't leave me alone here," Lydia said as she ran to Jaxson and took his hand. "Come on." She pulled him along while keeping the wolf in her sight. "It's hurt. We can catch it."

***

The wolf moved faster than Lydia or Jaxson could keep up with, but it took several breaks along the way. Time to set the doll down and let out a high-pitched whine before moving on. It was in those moments of pause that Lydia and Jaxson could bridge the gap and keep the animal in their sight.

The pursuit led them deep into the woods. Far beyond any distance Lydia had traveled before, she could sense Jaxson's reluctance growing with every step. Although Jaxson would rather have stayed behind in the first place, when the wolf scampered into a looming wall of fog, he all but insisted they give up the chase.

Lydia did not heed his warning, and she did not break her pace. The wolf was a blur, and she knew that if she hesitated for even a moment, it would vanish. "There's fog all over this town."

"This fog is different," Jaxson insisted, his words coming out in quick gasps as he struggled to keep up. "We need to turn back."

Lydia plunged through the fog. She did not wait for Jaxson, who was still shouting about the hazy veil hiding the true nature of what went on in the woods. His story did not scare her. What scared her was having to face the swamplands without her doll. After what she had seen today, she knew there was no hope of a future, cursed or otherwise, without Sophie.

She squinted, tracking the faint outline of the wolf as it continued to flee, hopping over cypress knees and splashing through the marsh. Every so often, the wolf looked back, its ears flattening against its head as it realized she was still in pursuit. Shortly after its last pause, the wolf dug its paws into the ground and took off, whimpering as it forced itself to sprint at speeds no human could match.

Lydia quickened her pace, calling for Jaxson to keep up, and wondering if he had followed. The wolf had already disappeared into the densening fog, leaving nothing but a blanket of white in front of her eyes. Obstacles were like phantoms, appearing out of nowhere just before she would have collided with them, forcing her to change course repeatedly.

The fog grew denser the further she ran, and the trees closed in around her. There was another shadow every moment, and she dodged each one, until a low-hanging branch appeared in front of her face. Its sharp wooden splinters pierced the flesh of her cheek, causing her head to snap backwards while her legs launched out from under her.

A minute or so later, Jaxson appeared and pulled her to her feet. "You're some kind of trouble," he said, as he sniffed the air.

Lydia took a deep breath through her nose, inhaling the smell of torched wood, and reigniting the memory of her parents. Someone was out there. The scent guided their path, and as she and Jaxson drew nearer, the crackle of the flames grew louder. Past the thick tree line ahead, they spotted a clearing with a shack nestled in the middle.

"The woman in the woods." Lydia said as she knelt behind a stump, peering out at the raging fire burning beside the home. "This must be where she lives. I think she's... my aunt."

Jaxson crouched beside her. "Where did the wolf go?"

"No idea." Lydia peered out from behind the

stump. "But the woman can help us get Sophie back."

"Now hold on," Jaxson said, grabbing the back of her shirt. "That woman ain't right."

Lydia slipped out of his grasp. "Wait here," she said. "If anything goes wrong, I'll call for you."

With that, Lydia left the stump behind and stepped out into the clearing. Up close, she could see that the woman's shack was poorly constructed. Its neglected appearance suggested that the woman had built it with little guidance or knowledge. Warped panels hung from rotted logs, creating a nightmarish appearance, and a poorly hung door groaned ominously on its hinges.

Lydia hurried across the porch, hoping the wooden boards would not break beneath her feet. She knocked, but there was no answer. Peering through the gap where the door and its frame should have met, she glimpsed the shack's interior and confirmed there was no one home.

She considered waiting for the woman to return. However, taking a moment to contemplate Jaxson's view reassessed the situation. What if the woman was a threat? It would be best for her to gather whatever information she could while she had the chance. And since there were no locks barring her from entering the shack, she pushed the door open and stepped inside.

At once, the smell of smoke was replaced by the

familiar aroma of herbs and musk, reminiscent of Mama's house. It was not the scent that held Lydia's attention captive, however. As she looked around, her eyes were immediately drawn to a table draped in a worn cloth and covered with a collection of yellow newspaper clippings. Collecting such items was no small task, as no paper route existed, and these papers appeared to come from several states' presses. The woman had to have ventured far from her shack to gather these, showcasing her unique ability to defy the Lurker's influence. And the newspaper headlines reinforced Lydia's suspicions. They appeared to follow a timeline of her father's life.

Family Loses Daughter to Hurricane.

Murder-Suicide Leaves Young Boy Orphaned.

Then, there was a wanted poster some years later.

Richard Kent, $5,000 Reward.

Lydia was sure of it now. The girl who was supposedly lost in the hurricane was her aunt. Per the second article, Lydia's grandparents left town after losing her aunt, and a short time later, her grandfather shot her grandmother before turning the gun on himself. In the third article, her orphaned father became a criminal. No wonder he did not want to call himself a Kent. It all aligned with what she had learned about the Lurker and the consequences people face when they try to leave town.

Nothing, however, gave Lydia concern about the woman's intentions until her eyes landed on a stack of crudely drawn sketches, revealing her aunt's unsettling and macabre nature. The images were horrifying—children suspended above roaring fires like the one burning outside, gripping tightly onto dolls. Ghostly silhouettes accompanied the children, who all appeared to be in great distress, their faces filled with such lifelike anguish, and beside them all, was the wolf.

A loud thud sounded as if something had struck the wall behind Lydia. She turned, her eyes searching the window, but there was no sign of movement or sound beyond the glass. Attributing the interruption to a misguided bird or fallen exterior panel, she continued to parse through the drawings. Written on the opposite side of each disturbing image were intricate notes in an unfamiliar script. Pictures of herbs were stenciled alongside the alien tongue, as if these images were pages belonging to a book of ritual or spells.

Another loud thud echoed through the shack, reverberating off the walls. Then a third. Startled by the shattering of glass, Lydia turned again and saw a rock tumbling towards her. Jaxson must be calling her back, she realized, collecting the drawings to bring with her.

She hated to admit it, but it appeared he was right. The woman's ability to travel and survive alone in the woods was not a result of defying the Lurker. Rather, it appeared to be a privilege the Lurker granted the woman for executing its will—torturing and killing children, perhaps even summoning her long-lost brother back to face judgment.

Lydia rushed to the door, her heart pounding as she imagined being suspended above the flames like the children in the drawings. She ran outside, but it was too late. The woman stood on the opposite side of the door, her vacant eyes fixed on Lydia, while the wolf sat obediently beside her, clenching Sophie in its violent jaws.

The Axe

Jaxson

From behind the stump, Jaxson watched helplessly, questioning why he had let Lydia drag him into this mess. He knew better than to venture off into the fog, where the air hung as heavy as his conscience. Before meeting Lydia, there was no circumstance that could have made him defy his father, but there was something about her presence which spoke to his soul.

She was a defiant girl to be sure, challenging the authority and wisdom of her elders, yet she was the purest person he had ever met. While the kids he had known for years shunned him, she saw beyond his curse and treated him with kindness. Perhaps that was why he followed her into the fog, despite his better instincts, and why he found himself consumed with the need to save her from the madwoman's grasp.

Now in front of the fire, Jaxson witnessed the woman raise her skeletal arm, releasing a fine, powdery substance that wafted over Lydia, causing Lydia's expression to shift from fear to submission. The woman gently pried Lydia's doll from the wolf's jaws, raising it above her head as she marched in circles around the flames. Entranced, Lydia followed behind the woman, her footsteps steady and even, with the wolf silently shadowing her.

Jaxson knew he had to be strategic and calculate his every move, making sure he remained unseen until he could grab Lydia. He scanned the area for any source of commotion that could divert the attention of her captors, and his eyes landed on a decaying tree. From the looks of it, the tree had been uprooted long ago. Remaining vertical, it hung precariously from the twisted branches of its neighbors. If he could dislodge the tree and cause it to fall, the resounding crash would draw their attention long enough for him to make his move.

He carefully ascended an adjacent tree, his arms hugging the rough bark as he inched higher. The woman and her wolf were still with Lydia, though the woman was dancing along with the flames now, and chanting words he had never heard. The flames rose higher, while the wolf's mournful howls filled the air.

As strange as it was, the noise provided Jaxson with leniency in his breathing and shuffling. When at last he reached the tangled branches and was rearing up to kick through them, a sharp hissing sound gave him pause.

Below his position, two gators shuffled by, inexplicably drawn into the mesmerizing ritual. Judging by their bloodstained jaws and the distended belly of the rightmost gator, he surmised that these were the same gators who had attacked earlier, carrying Maggie's partially digested remains within them. Distracting the woman and her wolf was one thing, but two man-eating reptiles made the already deadly mission seem futile.

With each chant, the woman's movements flowed effortlessly, her unintelligible words gaining a stronger rhythm. She tossed more handfuls of powder into the fire, which seemed to grow ever stronger and brighter, while Jaxson descended the tree to reconsider his plan. He lowered himself onto the ground, and as he did, the surrounding air grew thicker, and the putrid aroma of charred leather filled his nostrils, making him gag.

Two more visitors broke through the tree line. These two were human, at least they used to be. Jaxson could only assume the horrid-looking figures lumbering past him were the charred remains of Lydia's parents. The idea of the sorcery needed to conjure such an unholy thing made Jaxson shudder, but it all fed back to the woman in the woods. It was as if she were summoning the energy of everything Lydia's doll had encountered, and every trace of misfortune attached.

For what purpose, Jaxson could not fathom, but he knew the doll must belong to the woman, and she in turn must serve the Lurker.

Fortunately, Lydia's parents moved past him on a fixed path, completely unaware of his presence or even their own existence. The woman was gearing up for something sinister, something which could only spell trouble. Jaxson exhaled through his nose, feeling the weight of every precious moment slipping away. He knew he had to act. To save Lydia, he needed to find his father, and pray they made it back before the woman completed her ritual, so without wasting another moment, he ran home.

***

"Pa, where are you?"

Jaxson peeked into his father's room, squinting to make out any shapes in the pitch-blackness, and hoping to detect a hint of motion, but finding none. He got the sinking feeling that his father was out looking for him, as it was unusual for anyone in town to venture out at night without good cause. If he were right, then there was no use in wasting more time; Lydia's life was on the line.

Gathering his courage, Jaxson defied another of

his father's rules and made his way to the shed behind their cottage. He lit their kerosene lantern and, casting its firelight on the walls, searched for his father's woodchopping axe. He spotted the axe hanging on the far wall and snatched it off its rungs. Then he retrieved the lantern and headed out, hoping its flickering light would overpower the dark.

As he ran back to the woman's shack, the forested shadows lining his path seemed to grow, looming over him from every direction, intensifying his sense of unease. Damp air clung to his skin, and a peculiar electric tang filled his mouth. The lantern swung back and forth in his left hand, while he dragged the weighty axe behind in his right, carving a path into the mud behind him.

Looking back, he noticed faint sparks of lightning dancing above the swamp, their static discharge filling his ears like a distant radio receiver. A symphony of splashes followed the sparks, accompanied by the unmistakable chorus of frogs whose usually melodious calls were replaced with piercing cries of warning. They knew what Jaxson knew. The Lurker was stalking the area, concealing its presence in the gloom, and mirroring Jaxson's movements from the still waters. Jaxson bit down on his lip, the taste of warm blood spilling into his mouth as he pushed himself harder.

When Jaxson plunged through the wall of fog,

he was relieved to feel the static dissipate. It was as if his visitor had retreated, unwilling to leave the murky waters. Shortly ahead, the woman's clearing emerged, well illuminated by the ritualistic fire, which was still burning strong. Jaxson slid in between the towering trees and set his lantern behind the stump. He breathed a sigh of relief upon seeing that Lydia was still alive but soon realized she might not be that way for long.

The woman had bound Lydia to a stake and suspended her in front of the roaring pyre. Lydia's wide-open eyes were transfixed, as though her mind had disconnected from her physical body. She had undoubtedly fallen prey to the same sorcery that Jaxson's father feared.

Flames licked at her clothing, drawing no reaction from her. The hissing gators, howling wolf, and Lydia's parents, whose burned flesh had fractured and fallen to the ground, were gathered around the fire in formation. Meanwhile, the woman continued her dance, unaware of Jaxson's stealthy approach.

When Jaxson drew near enough, he stood tall, feeling the weight of the axe in his hands, and with a swift motion, he swung it at the woman. The blade lodged itself in her skull, causing her knees to buckle and her lifeless body to collapse onto the ground.

Horrified by what he had done, Jaxson took a step

back and watched the morbid scene unravel. Without the woman's influence, Lydia's parents fell like puppets cut from their strings, their bodies crumpling into a heap of charred flesh. The gators' reptilian instincts returned as they sprinted away, primal nature urging them to seek refuge in the familiar embrace of the swamp.

Even so, the wolf remained. A devoted servant, to be forever marred by the memory of its master's death. With mournful whines and desperate yelps, the beast's sorrow overwhelmed its aggression, granting Jaxson the time to needed to dislodge the axe from the woman's skull and examine Lydia's restraints.

Lydia's eyes began to shift and wander as he surveyed the thick ropes binding her, and they grew wide when he lined up his axe. He swung carefully, however, severing the ropes where they met the stake, and causing Lydia to fall safely to the ground.

"What did she do to you?" Jaxson asked, rushing to her side.

Lydia's dazed eyes wandered from the slain woman over to her parents' blackened skeletons and finally met Jaxson's gaze. "I'm not sure."

Jaxson shifted, blocking Lydia's view of her parents as he guided her away from the gruesome pile. "I told you not to go past the fog," he said, as he looked back at the corpses. "This isn't right; none of it. Pa's going to kill me for coming here. I can't believe I took his axe, and I..."

"You were helping me." Lydia spotted her doll on the ground and ran for it. "It's not your fault. The woman stole Sophie, and we were getting her back."

"No more dolls," Jaxson said, tightening his grip on the axe. "Set it down so I can take care of it."

Lydia's face contorted. "I won't."

The wolf's eyes locked onto Lydia. Looking up from its slain master, the wolf's whines transformed into a deep growl. Jaxson pivoted, his body tense as he positioned himself between Lydia and the wolf, prepared to strike if necessary. Together, he and Lydia backed away, and as they retreated, he snatched up his lantern. The wolf continued to growl, watching intently, though it did not follow them past the trees.

"The beast won't stop." Jaxson turned to Lydia. "The doll belongs to its master."

"Does not." Lydia fixed him with a menacing stare. "Sophie saved us."

"Nobody needed saving until you showed up with that doll. Set it down and stand back."

Lydia stood firm. "I won't."

An unsettling glow illuminated Lydia's face, casting a ghostly green hue on their surroundings. Followed by wind, which whipped through the trees, bringing with it an unseasonable chill that stole the fog from the air. With the veil lifted, the Lurker's haunting static crackled in the background.

Jaxson paused, his eyes scanning their transforming environment, which seemed to mirror Lydia's dire mood. It was not she who gripped the doll with all her might; it was the doll which held an unwavering hold over her. Even in death, the woman's black magic held a power which lingered, a persistence fed by the Lurker who had followed him. Jaxson reached out his hand, yearning for Lydia to release the doll, but deep down, he knew it was a futile hope.

"No." Lydia took a step back, her eyes igniting with a disturbing and intense energy.

"It's just a doll," Jaxson pleaded. "Leave it."

Lydia became frantic. "I need her," she stammered. "Sophie. She loves me."

Jaxson watched as Lydia's breath quickened, her chest rising and falling like a jackhammer. The harder she breathed, the harder she clung to her doll, and the harder she clung, the more the world around them twisted. Felled moss lifted from the ground, swept up in a cyclone of intensifying winds which swirled around them. Electrical pulses crackled and fizzled in the air, sweeping through the woods, and feeding into the doll, consuming Lydia with its energy.

Jaxson lunged for her but was cut short by an electrified bolt. It surged from the doll and collided with the head of his axe, creating a blinding flash which threw him to the ground. His body convulsed. He tried to stand, but every muscle fiber screamed in torment. As he struggled, another surge electrified the air, sending him back to the ground. His pain abruptly ceased as darkness consumed his vision.

The Void

Lydia

Even in the warmth of Mama LeFleur's home, Lydia's heart ached. Last night, after making sure that Jaxson had survived the shock, she left him there in the woods, fearful of what would unfold if she stayed. Would he have persisted in destroying her doll, even if it meant endangering both of their lives? As she arrived home, that question lingered at the forefront of her mind, keeping her awake long after she snuck into her bed.

She rose late the next morning to the sound of Mama LeFleur's tea kettle, feeling drowsy but glad to be back in the comfort of Mama's house. Fortunately, Mama's concern for her wellbeing outweighed any disappointment, earning her sympathy, but the good fortune ended there.

The woman's ritual had stolen something from Lydia, leaving a void where there should have been a feeling. During the lightning storm, Lydia felt a sudden detachment from her doll, and afterwards, that sense of disconnect only intensified. It was as if she had lost a piece of her identity during the ritual.

She could no longer feel the doll's soft body against her fingertips, gaze into its lifelike eyes, and find solace in the belief that everything would be alright. If the doll was supposed to be her protector, then why did it not intervene when the woman in the woods performed her ritual, and why would it hurt Jaxson?

Mama LeFleur set a small cup on the table in front of Lydia. "Have some tea, child."

Lydia placed her doll next to the teacup, observing how its lifeless body crumpled under the strain of its heavy head. Its eyes, once filled with magic and enchantment, now seemed vacant, their bright blue color dulled and lifeless. As Lydia stared at the doll, her fists clenched, and her body shook. She leaned in closer, holding her breath as she searched for signs of life. Anything. A flicker of blue in its dead eyes, or a touch of green emanating from its body. Any glimmer of hope which could usher her through the overwhelming darkness.

"Is Jaxson going to be okay?"

"Jaxson's a sturdy boy," Mama said. "He'll be shaken, but I'm sure he's fine."

"Sorry again for running off." Lydia looked up at Mama. "My Sophie," she said, her voice trembling as she fought to hold back her tears, "doesn't feel like she did before."

"Nothing a cup of tea can't fix," Mama insisted.

Lydia gave in and took a sip from her teacup, hoping it would be enough to appease Mama. Although Lydia was hesitant, the warm, earthy liquid brought some comfort. Its heat spread through her body and eased the tension in her muscles.

She thought about the other children her age from the city where she used to live. How they must be getting ready to spend their summer days at the playground while she sat inside Mama's house, drinking tea to relieve the tension of a day that would have scarred them for life.

Until now, Lydia's doll had kept her emotions at bay, but with their connection severed, negativity crept in, making the world feel darker and heavier. She took a deep breath, closing her eyes as she finished the last of her tea, and savoring the relief it brought.

Mama smiled, taking Lydia's hand in hers, and with her other hand, Mama took hold of the doll. Lydia watched with confusion as Mama closed her eyes and spoke in a language she could not understand. After a minute of this talk had passed, Lydia felt a shift in her predicament. The air was electric, and the doll glowed again, filling her with a sense of comfort and familiarity. Her intrusive thoughts faded, and her memories softened, allowing her to exist in the present.

Lydia held the doll close to her heart. "How did you..."

"The woman you met was powerful," Mama LeFleur said as she shifted in her seat. "By gathering everything your doll touched, well... You're from the big city. Picture those new electric streetlights they got. Give them too much power and they'll explode. The woman recognized your connection to the doll and tried to destroy it in much the same way."

"Did she serve the Lurker?"

Mama LeFleur nodded, and sensing Lydia's thoughts, responded, "You don't have to worry about the doll, child. I promise she's okay now. After all, I made her just for you."

Lydia felt a shiver crawl up her back. "You made her?"

"In my workshop," Mama said.

"Why haven't you said so?" Lydia asked. "The Sheriff turned Jaxson against Sophie."

"The Sheriff still blames his sister's doll for what happened all those years ago, so I kept quiet, letting the dolls remain a mystery. Trust me, if Elijah knew I was making them, he'd burn me at the stake."

Mama opened up about the Lurker after that, sharing details that confirmed many of the things Lydia had already learned. The Lurker was believed to be a scapegoat for the horrible tragedies which befell the town, but Mama knew better than the non-believers.

The Lurker was undeniably real; a creature not bound by the laws of this world. Its influence, the result of an electrical current it exuded, was a valuable resource that Mama and the woman in the woods learned to harness, one for good and the other for evil.

Mama's detailed description of the Lurker made Lydia nauseous, especially when she detailed the writhing arms extending from its lumpy center mass, like oily serpents ready to strike. Despite its physical prowess, however, the Lurker's greatest weapon was its ability to manipulate the minds of its prey, a power that extended to the flora and fauna of the town, including its residents. Mama explained the Lurker had the freedom to leave the swamp, but only for so long as it breathed through gills, which sat atop the lumpy mounds of flesh comprising its center of mass.

Lydia's imagination got the best of her as she attempted to picture the electrical creature, pondering its origins and intentions. "You can make a doll to protect Jaxson, then," she said.

Mama LeFleur shook her head. "Jaxson was born here; he doesn't need a doll."

"He does." Lydia jumped to her feet. "If the dolls protect people from the Lurker's influence, then Jaxson needs one. Especially after last night. I can help you make it."

"The boy can't have one," Mama LeFleur remained firm. "I don't believe he needs one either. I've suspected the Sheriff to be a servant for some time, and it won't be long before the boy joins him. The only cursed people are the ones who spend time with them."

"But—"

"No buts, child." Mama LeFleur collected Lydia's teacup and walked it to the counter. "I won't hear another word of it," she said, returning to the table. "That woman's ritual is like a virus in your system. I need you to rest up. You'll be just fine by tomorrow."

Lydia retreated to her bedroom, dove under the covers, and muffled her cries in the softness of her pillow. The past night's events replayed in her mind, consuming her thoughts, until she re-directed her focus. Silently, she promised to seize control of her situation.

Mama may disapprove of Jaxson having a doll, but in Lydia's mind, he deserved one. Everyone did. The thought of being the only child in town with protection from the Lurker was wrong. Maggie's death served as proof that no one, local or otherwise, was exempt from danger.

To help Jaxson and earn his forgiveness, she needed to share what she learned about the Lurker and craft a doll for him. The only problem was that she did not know how. Mama mentioned a workshop, but she had never seen one. She reasoned it was hidden somewhere in the vicinity, and Jaxson was going to help her find it.

The Abandoned House

Lydia

"Jaxson, slow down!" Lydia shouted, gasping for breath.

She kicked clumps of mud behind her with each stride, flinging them across the marsh in a shower of wet earth as she ran towards the water's edge. Jaxson quickened his pace, however. Transitioning from a jog into a sprint, unwilling to hear a word she had to say.

"I didn't mean to hurt you." Lydia gritted her teeth and pushed harder, her legs churning as she caught up with Jaxson and tackled him. "I learned something yesterday," she panted.

Jaxson lay defeated on the muddy bank, his clothes soaked and caked with dirt. "Leave me alone," he said, averting his gaze. "You're nothing but trouble."

"We're in danger, Jaxson." Lydia caught her breath. "But the dolls can help."

Jaxson sat up, crossing his arms over his chest. "Your stupid doll just about killed me."

"It was the woman. She messed with the current

and made Sophie go bad, but Mama fixed her. I can help you now. We can help the town. We just need to find Mama's workshop."

"You sound crazy." Jaxson shook his head. "No way."

Lydia leaned in close to his ear, leery of anyone or anything that might be listening in on their conversation. "Mama made Sophie."

Jaxson's shaky breathing hinted at his mixed emotions towards Mama LeFleur, and her potential involvement with the doll. He was more trusting and less combative than his father, but he could not fully shake the Sheriff's deep-rooted influence on him or the resulting duality within himself.

While trying to convince Jaxson to help her make more dolls, Lydia realized just how far the Sheriff's influence reached. Not only did Jaxson believe whole-heartedly in the curse that plagued his family, but he also believed that Lydia was cursed too, and that Mama LeFleur was a senile old woman who played with forces she did not understand and who could be responsible for his aunt's disappearance.

Although Jaxson's beliefs were no stranger than her own, Lydia felt Jaxson was lacking something she possessed. Trust that the future held promise, and faith in the integrity of people. She embraced the idea that good is always present, even when it is overshadowed by bad, and felt if people stopped running and hiding from the Lurker, or denying its existence, they could stand up and reclaim their power.

"You're sure Mama made your doll?" Jaxson asked, his voice filled with uncertainty. "I've never seen a workshop. Barely seen Mama leave home."

"Mama wouldn't lie to me."

"And I can't have one," he said, trying to understand Mama's reasoning. "Maybe the dolls are too powerful to have more than one, or they stop working, or they go bad. You think about that?"

"Better than everyone getting eaten."

Jaxson froze, no doubt recollecting what had become of Maggie.

Lydia softened her tone. "Whose house was I under when we met?" she asked. "It looked like it was abandoned."

"It's my pa's old place."

"So, it's supposed to be empty…" Lydia pondered. "No one would know if Mama was in there."

Jaxson cocked his head. "Nobody has set foot inside there since my aunt went missing all those years ago." He swallowed hard, no doubt realizing what Lydia's next request would be. "It's locked up good," he said. "Forbidden."

Despite Jaxson's objection, she caught a glint in his eyes, a silent confirmation he would not let her enter the abandoned house alone, and that was all she needed. "I'll sneak out after Mama goes to sleep," she said, rising to her feet. "You give your dad the slip and meet me there. I bet that's Mama's workshop."

***

The nice thing about staying with Mama LeFleur was that Lydia could come and go as she pleased without fear of consequence. She used Mama's trust to her advantage, sneaking out with her doll as soon as the sun dipped beneath the reach of the forest. The sky was deep orange, and the trees looked like silhouetted ghosts with their moss swaying in the evening breeze.

Despite the relative warmth, a shiver ran down Lydia's spine as she took in the orange and black lines reflected on the surface of the swamp. She kept a brisk pace; navigating through the looming darkness was the biggest challenge of leaving at this hour.

Unlike the lit city streets that she grew up around, the swamplands were shrouded in darkness. Most light was hidden by twisted trees, and the fireflies, despite their beautiful glow, did little to guide her way. By the time she arrived at the abandoned house, the sun had set, and only the dim glow of the moon lit the house's front porch, leaving the doors and windows barely visible beneath a swath of foreboding shadow.

Lydia's heart raced as she heard a terrible dragging sound behind her. She turned sharply, fearing the worst. But it was only Jaxson, dragging his father's axe behind him and carrying his unwieldy steel lantern in the other hand. Jaxson's expression was solemn as he walked past her up to the porch, where he leaned the axe against a rotted wooden beam.

"Smart thinking," Lydia said, thankful they had a light source.

Jaxson nodded to her slowly and deliberately, as if he were holding something back. "You really want to go in there?" he asked, pointing his lantern at the house.

As she watched the shadows play across Jaxson's face, Lydia's gaze drifted to the moonlit mist, and then to the murky waters beyond the house. This town was not her chosen home, but it was hers now, and protecting it from the Lurker was her duty. Like Mama said, sometimes it takes a pinch of sunshine. She could not live her whole life in fear, knowing nothing but loss, when the solution was waiting for them, and if her intuition was correct, waiting just beyond that door.

Lydia nodded back at Jaxson, her heart beating faster with anticipation. She tossed her doll onto the porch and grabbed Jaxson's axe on her way up the stairs, feeling its rough, splintering wooden handle beneath her fingers. The yellow light of the lantern flickered on the blade like a mirror, casting an eerie glow on its bloodstained edge.

She closed her eyes, attempting to purge the chilling images that plagued her mind—the woman's severed skull, Maggie Dupont's headless body, and her parents in their various stages of char and decay. As she breathed through the memories, she tightened her grip on the axe's handle and lifted it high above her head. With a primal scream, she brought it down with all her strength, rattling the front door.

She stepped back, wincing at the pain from the force of the blow. Heat welled inside her chest, a physical manifestation of her troubled thoughts. She took another deep breath, then battered the door relentlessly until the wood around the lock cracked and splintered. With a final blow, she knocked the lock off the door, and it swung open. The home's interior exuded a smell Lydia could not make sense of. A pungent blend of musty mold and a metallic tang, underscored by a faintly sweet aroma buried deep within the decay.

Jaxson plugged his nose as he joined her on the stoop, lifting his lantern into the black void beyond the doorframe. The fire did little to illuminate the innards of the dwelling, which held a darkness so black it looked as though they were about to enter an underground cave.

Lydia peered into the shadows, her heart continuing to pound with fear at what might lie ahead. This was, after all, the vile place where she spotted the disturbance in the waters, a rotten upheaval that could only have come from an otherworldly entity.

The house exhaled a gust of frigid air, which made her skin tighten. She nudged Jaxson's hand, interlocking her pinky finger with his as she tried to settle her nerves. Jaxson shivered in turn, his eyes fixed straight ahead, refusing to meet her gaze, as if he were trying to deny his own fear.

Tossing the axe aside, Lydia stepped into the darkness alongside him, feeling the chilly, damp air enveloping her. Their lantern flickered out in an instant, plunging them into total darkness. Then the door shut behind them, and a faint hum started in. The closer they got to the center of the home, the stronger the humming became, until it felt like a physical presence pushing in on them from all sides.

Lydia tightened her pinky finger around Jaxson's, realizing her doll was still sitting on the porch outside. Before she could turn back, lights phased on all around them, and they found themselves surrounded by an army of dolls. On dilapidated shelves they sat, toppled over, and leaned against one another, as if huddling for warmth. Some were so old their clothing was all but fully deteriorated. The faint glow of each doll illuminated the darkness, however, creating a haunting ambience as they hummed in perfect harmony.

Lydia took a doll off its shelf. "This isn't a workshop; it's a warehouse."

"Who cares?" Jaxson shifted uncomfortably. "There are so many dolls. Where are their people?"

"Do you think their powers work for anyone?" Lydia asked.

"I don't know, but they've all got something on them. Like yours," he said. "It wears your bow."

Lydia recalled her doll's bow. She knew it was identical to hers, but she never considered that it *was* hers. The haunting tingle returned to her spine, and she felt a wave of unease wash over her body. She had lost some bows while playing in the marsh, just after moving to town, which meant Mama LeFleur had retrieved them well before their introduction.

Such peculiarities were not out of character for Mama. The old woman spoke freely of the world beyond and made no secret of dabbling in sorcery. Lydia reminded herself that her doll had been a reliable source of help thus far, and that these dolls were much like hers, holding the power to save the town. Whatever Mama had done, Lydia trusted, was done for good. What she did not know was why these dolls were stocked in the abandoned Hayes' house, who they belonged to prior to their arrival, or how they still hummed with the same magic as hers.

No matter what the scenario, Jaxson needed a doll. As did the rest of the town's kids. If she could harness the power of the existing dolls by attaching clothing or jewelry to them, she would not need to make new ones. She perused the overstuffed shelving units, hoping to begin with a suitable doll for Jaxson, but was drawn to a sparkle coming from the corner of the room.

The light emanated from within a small chest, beckoning her like a siren's call. She placed the doll she was holding on the ground and reached out to touch the rusty lock sealing the chest, its corroded surface left a gritty residue on her fingers. Then a small electric shock ran through her fingertips, causing her grip to tighten around the lock. As she pulled her hand back, she felt the lock release, granting her access to the chest and a brightly glowing doll that was trapped inside.

"This one looks like you," she said, turning to Jaxson.

"That's a girl," Jaxson replied, before he considered. "It's dressed like an old portrait of my aunt." He paced about the room, visibly shaken by the likeness. "I have to show my pa."

"We can't trust him," Lydia snapped, recalling Mama's suspicions about the Sheriff. She knew Jaxson did not serve the Lurker, but his father's allegiances were questionable, and this doll was special.

"He's my pa." Jaxson grabbed the doll and yanked it. "Give it to me."

Lydia lost her grip, causing her to stumble backward and take out a low-hanging shelf. Several dolls fell, one headfirst, shattering the fragile material and releasing a dazzling burst of light. As the light was sucked from the room, the sound of a ghostly whistle echoed through their ears, sending chills down their spines.

Darkness descended upon them like a heavy blanket as the dolls' lights faded. The floorboards shook violently and cracked. Then came the sound Lydia had been dreading since they arrived. The Lurker's drone permeated the air, rising above the toxic sludge of the bubbling swamp outside, until it screamed at them like Mama's boiling kettle. The sound reverberated within their heads, driving them to the brink of madness. They tried to escape, but the front door was being held shut by an unknown force.

Jaxson's frustration boiled over. He began kicking and punching at the front door with all his might, hoping to break through its inexplicable seal. Meanwhile, Lydia spotted an old rocking chair in the corner and dragged it to the window. Together, she and Jaxson flung the chair into the window frame. The wooden grid gave way with a satisfying crack, displacing the remnants of shattered glass as it fell.

Jaxson leapt over the sill with his new doll, waiting on the other side to help Lydia. She planted her foot on the sill and grabbed Jaxson's hands, allowing him to pull her through. Then she snatched her doll from the porch and sprinted after Jaxson, never daring to look back and face the Lurker.

The Dilemma

Jaxson

Once he was sure they had left the Lurker behind, Jaxson parted ways with Lydia, his mind still racing with adrenaline from their escape. More than that, his heart raced when he contemplated what to do with the doll in his hands.

Beacon of untold evil or friend, he wondered, unable to deny that the doll bore a striking resemblance to his aunt's portrait. To be a dutiful son, he knew he had to tell his father about everything he had done, where he had been, and the unsettling discovery he had made. Despite knowing this was the proper course of action, he struggled to follow through with it, fearing his father's reaction.

Nothing brought light to his father's eyes, not since Jaxson's mother had left them. Even before that, the light never fully graced his father's expression. There was always emptiness in his stare, and it stood to reason that, as far as Jaxson was concerned, the only thing which could bring his father joy was the return of his sister. Maybe then they could be an actual family. He had witnessed what normal family bonds looked like, in the eyes of the children around town, when they spoke proudly to one another about their parents and the times they shared. It was all Jaxson wanted, and sometimes all he could think about.

Although shackled with a singular perspective since birth, Jaxson knew his situation was peculiar, shunning his neighbors for fear he would poison them with his affliction. He could not help but wonder what it would be like to wake up without the constant weight of this curse on his shoulders.

Such thoughts had never crossed his mind until Lydia showed up, and he finally got to experience what it was like to have a sense of normalcy. As an outsider who saw him for who he was, Lydia treated him well, and despite her eccentricities, she seemed to have a genuine concern for his well-being. Maybe that was why he followed her lead, getting into new kinds of trouble and risking his own skin, all for the hope that life would get better.

At home, Jaxson quietly placed the doll in front of his father's bedroom door, knowing that his father would not be able to give it his full consideration if he were startled awake. It was imperative Jaxson placed the doll now, however, or he would risk losing his nerve and miss out on the opportunity to solve a mystery that had been plaguing his life for as long as he could remember.

Exhausted and overwhelmed, Jaxson retreated to his room and buried himself under the covers, tossing and turning, as his mind replayed the horrific drone of the Lurker. Although he had lived in the Lurker's shadow his entire life, the creature was mythical to Jaxson, always just out of reach.

Tonight marked a sobering change. The Lurker was no longer just a bedtime story, or the bearer of their curse. It was a tangible threat, which he had to face. He could not help but wonder about the depth of their intertwined history and what secrets lay behind his father's broken gaze. Whatever they were, he prayed for answers come morning, though he did not sleep until dawn's first light.

The Solution

Lydia

Lydia's gaze was fixed on the glassy eye of a lifeless alligator, swaying gently by its tail from an oak tree. Another gator dangled next to it, its scales shimmering with a crimson trail of blood. Jaxson's loose lips must have revealed the finer details of Maggie's passing, which the Sheriff then shared with the townsfolk.

Although she could tell these were not the gators responsible for Maggie Dupont's death, the residents cared little about such details. In memoriam, a few of the town's younger men had hunted down the first two gators they could find and strung them up, so their bodies could provide a spectacle. The townsfolk would gather under them soon to mourn Maggie's passing by candlelight, which gave Lydia the opportunity she needed to be in close contact with all the town's children.

Mama's dolls needed to be dressed in their garments so that Lydia could test her theory, and with clouds swallowing the evening sky, her time was running out. The storm Mama warned her about was coming. She had to gather all the belongings she could without being noticed, then leave before creating a stir. Once she swiped an item from each of the kids, she planned to return to the abandoned house and dress several dolls, ensuring to choose dolls which closely resembled their human counterparts.

As the crowd arrived for Maggie's vigil, Lydia made herself scarce, disappearing into the dense undergrowth of cattails and shrubbery. If there was one thing she learned from questioning the townsfolk about the Lurker, it was that many of them were not fond of outsiders under the best of circumstances. Not even the kids she was trying to help showed any decency towards her, prompting her to hide until sunset, when she could discreetly snatch their possessions under the cover of darkness.

Before long, the town had gathered, their candles were lit, and the overcast sky had gone dark. Lydia noticed a young girl sitting alone, her back turned, and acted. With a deft hand, she passed by the girl and lifted the decorative bow from her hair before disappearing behind a tree trunk. Puzzled, the girl patted her head, turning in every direction before giving up and stomping off to tell her parents.

Lydia shifted her attention towards a boy whose

hat flew from his head as he chased after his friend. She snatched the hat from the ground before he knew it was missing, and she was gone by the time he returned. With each item she swiped, Lydia inched closer to her goal, but she could not ignore the growing awareness among the townspeople.

When she moved in on her next target, the atmosphere had grown tense. Her footsteps were silent on the ground, and her intention was to snatch the glasses from a boy who had his eyes closed, counting out loud for a round of hide and seek. It was a risky move, but she could not let any opportunity slip through her fingers. She reached around his head from behind, feeling the cool touch of the glasses before ripping them off in a swift motion. The gamble almost paid off, but a misplaced footstep sent her sprawling onto the ground.

"My dad's gonna kill me." The boy reached down, took his glasses back, and tried to bend the broken wire frame into place. "He had to go to the city to get these."

"Sorry." Lydia stood, brushing the dirt from her clothes. "Can you keep quiet? I'm trying to—"

"You're the one who's stealing everyone's stuff."

Before Lydia could argue, a lightning bolt crashed nearby, leaving her temporarily blinded. She blinked, and turning around, spotted a gang of disgruntled parents making their way towards her. One of them called her presence into question, pointing out that Lydia and her doll were the catalyst for Maggie's attack. Another parent accused her, rightly so, of stealing from their child and tarnishing the spirit of Maggie's vigil. Soon, the townspeople were converging on her, their angry voices growing louder with each step while burning rain fell from the sky.

Unease washed over Lydia as she realized that any one of these people could serve the Lurker, maybe even all of them. There was no telling what they would do in their current state of distress, vulnerable to the Lurker's manipulation.

Although she had not collected enough belongings to dress dolls for all the children, she needed to seek refuge somewhere safe, somewhere she knew the townspeople would not dare bother her. Mama's house. Mama commanded respect in the community, and her power was well known, so Lydia turned and sprinted away, leaving behind a cacophony of taunts and insults.

The Storm

Jaxson

Just before the vigil, Jaxson had woken from his off-cycle slumber, and looking out the window, realized that dusk was setting. Dark gray storm clouds had already devoured most of the sunlight as he sprung out of bed, feeling guilty for sleeping late, and wondering if his father was angry with him over the doll.

The living area was eerily quiet as he stepped out of his room. The liquor cabinet was open, and his father's chair was empty. Jaxson ran to his father's room and found that the doll was gone, leaving him to assume the worst. He knew his father was unstable, yet he left the doll for his father to find with no explanation, without considering that it could trigger an episode.

It was unlikely his father had gone to the vigil, as the townsfolk enjoyed keeping the Hayes at arm's length. But there was a surefire place Jaxson knew to check when life was not going well. Their fishing hole, where his father often nullified his isolation and pain over a drink. Jaxson dressed in a hurry and headed out the door, but when he reached the fishing hole where he was sure he would find his father, buried knee deep in the muck with a bottle of moonshine, there was no one.

The surrounding mud was untouched, save for Jaxson's footprints and the hurried tracks of animals seeking shelter from the brewing storm. It was then that Jaxson's concern for his father turned into genuine fear. He considered enlisting Lydia to help him in the search, but remembering her suspicions about his father, decided against it. There was no telling what conclusions Lydia might draw if she knew his father had disappeared with the doll.

Jaxson persisted in his search, scouring every inch of the town. He even stopped to observe the vigil from a distance, but ultimately, was left with only one location to consider. The one place he had hoped never to set foot in again. The abandoned house, with its creaky floorboards and cracked windows, filled with haunting dolls, and guarded by the Lurker, whose drone echoed incessantly in his mind.

The air crackled with a discomforting static hum as Jaxson approached the abandoned house, and his arms became battlefields of raised hairs, all of which were prepared for action. Chills swept through his tense muscles, priming his legs for a speedy retreat.

Despite his better judgment and flight instinct, Jaxson forced himself to push forward, and as he approached the far side of the abandoned home, he glimpsed his father's silhouette.

"Where are you, you no-good son of a bitch?" Sheriff Hayes shouted.

Jaxson sought cover behind the bark of a thick tree and peered out, wondering exactly who his father's rage was targeted at. Even from a distance, he could smell the alcohol lingering in the air, emanating from an empty bottle of moonshine on the ground. Reflected in the bottle was the faint glow of a doll. He could only assume his father had drawn the same conclusion he had about the doll. That it was, in fact, his aunt's doll, and that the Lurker was using it for something nefarious.

Sheriff Hayes picked a log off the ground and hurled it into the swamp. "Show yourself, dammit."

The swamp churned and bubbled, emitting a faint scent of sweetened rot as bright lines of plasma crackled over its murky surface. Jaxson plugged his ears to shield his mind from the Lurker's terrible drone. He could feel the cold, clammy touch of dread crawling up his spine as appendages reminiscent of snakes broke through the water's surface.

Rising water cascaded off the bulbous mass that followed, and Jaxson knew instantly that he was staring at the Lurker. Its appearance was lumpy and dark, with a smoky quartz-like transparency and a pink pulsating light emanating from within. Electric currents surged through the translucent creature, creating an ethereal glow that spread to the air and water.

The sky itself seemed to darken in response, as if the creature were casting its shadow upon the stars. When the Lurker had fully risen, it hovered above the swamp, revealing a globelike body with feelers stretching out in all directions.

"You said she was lost." The Sheriff's voice grew dim as he picked his sister's doll off the ground. "How long have you had her?"

The Lurker's glow intensified, and the smell of ozone filled the air as lightning tore through the night. With each electric pulse, the Lurker pulled the storm from the sky, unleashing its fury upon the marsh. The Lurker did not speak. It only droned and pulsed, yet the Sheriff seemed to understand its message, continuing to hurl drunken insults as torrential rains washed over him.

Jaxson hunkered down behind the tree. His body pressed against its rough surface as intense winds howled around him. He knew now that Lydia was right; his father served the Lurker, although unwillingly. Still, as Jaxson looked on, he could no longer ignore the truth. His family was not cursed. It was his father who brought misfortune upon them, no doubt chasing Jaxson's mother away with his madness.

With every unfiltered word his father hurled at the Lurker, Jaxson's understanding of the dolls and the Lurker deepened, and each sentence underscored the bleakness of their situation. A sickening feeling burrowed inside him when he learned the woman in the woods, whose skull he had severed, was no servant. The fog shielded her from the Lurker's influence, and in gathering all the life touched by Lydia's doll, she had hoped to conquer the Lurker's hold over Lydia.

Then something dawned on Jaxson—Mama LeFleur must also be corrupt. Which meant Lydia was alone with a monster, vulnerable to the growing storm. He retreated into the marsh, the drone of the Lurker fading behind him as he raced to save Lydia from Mama.

***

The storm relentlessly battled Jaxson, showering him with raindrops that stung like burning oil. He covered his face with his arm, shielding his eyes as he pushed onward. Dark clouds had stolen the stars from the sky, forcing him to rely on sporadic flashes of lightning to navigate the marsh. As he ran, howling winds ripped a wave of moss from a towering cypress tree, which descended on him like a net.

Jaxson broke free from its grasp and pressed on against a storm which seemed designed to stop him, while the town groaned under the strain of the downpour. Houses swayed on their stilts, threatening to collapse in on themselves, and branches reached out to grab Jaxson as he ran past. The relentless rumble of thunder reverberated through his bones, drowning out the smack of his feet as he trampled through rising mud puddles.

When Mama LeFleur's house came into view, he called out for Lydia, his voice trembling. He knew she was not safe at Mama's house, or in town. Neither of them was, but he would make sure they found refuge. He did not know where or how, only that he had to find somewhere. But before he could reach Mama's porch, a gust of wind knocked him off his feet.

Lydia walked outside, the doll dangling from her hand. "Are you okay?"

Jaxson stood. "Where's Mama LeFleur?"

"In bed," Lydia said, confusion written on her face.

"We need to leave town," Jaxson insisted. "Just you and me. The doll stays here."

Lydia planted her feet on the wet earth, undeterred by the mud seeping between her toes. Nor offput by the raindrops smacking her face. "We can't leave."

"We have to."

"No." Lydia stood resolutely against the storm, unblinking, as though she were questioning his sanity. "Come with me to the abandoned house. I've collected things to dress the dolls with."

Lydia's tone conveyed a deepening obsession. She was blissfully unaware of the dolls' purpose, but Jaxson had learned the horrible truth. Wherever the dolls went, they became conduits of destruction, expanding the Lurker's influence like signal amplifiers.

It did not need to be dolls. The Lurker could have crafted any hollow shape from that detestable alien material, as long as the resulting form held value in the hands of its victims. Disguised as protectors, the dolls' purpose was to unleash chaos, exploiting the fear they evoked to drain the life force from the children who clung to them.

"You don't understand." Jaxson moved closer, bringing himself within arm's reach of the doll. "That doll is stealing from you," he said, reaching out to her. "There's no beating the Lurker. We need to leave while we still can."

Lightning crashed overhead as his hand touched the doll, illuminating the disgust in Lydia's eyes. She did not trust him, nor could she. Not with the weight of the Lurker's influence pulling her deeper into its orbit and its servants leading her astray. Jaxson knew she would never surrender her doll willingly, but as her friend, he felt responsible for protecting her.

Lydia did not deserve the same fate as his aunt and the other trapped souls. Jaxson took hold of her doll and pulled, determined to take it from her, but Lydia clung tight. The storm grew stronger as they struggled, matching the intensity of their emotions as they each fought for possession of the doll.

"It's for your own good," Jaxson said, emerging victorious from the struggle.

Lydia, always a quiet girl, yelled at him in a voice he could hardly have imagined. "You can't have her!" And riding on the back of her words came an onslaught of lightning strikes.

The air was charged with electricity as the lightning storm drew nearer, culminating in a violent strike that exploded against a mighty cypress tree. The resulting thunder shook both children to their core, while the deafening sound left them disoriented.

Jaxson, his head still ringing from the Lurker's drone, was oblivious to the subsequent cracks which echoed through the air, signifying the immense pressure placed on the colossal cypress as its fibers shattered. The crackling grew louder and louder until a final resounding snap drew Jaxson's attention in time for him to turn. Looking up at the towering tree, his eyes filled with helplessness as it crashed down on him.

It Ends Tonight

Lydia

Lydia winced, feeling a rush of fear and helplessness as the massive tree crashed down on Jaxson. Mud erupted from the impact, shooting out in every direction. Reluctantly, she crept forward, her voice trembling as she called out to him, fearing the worst. To find him, she had to climb the massive trunk and peer down through its tangled mess of branches.

Jaxson was spared the full weight of the trunk, though he was thrown with force, leaving him pinned to the ground with a heavy gash through his head. She reached her arm down and shook him, but his lifeless body remained silent and still.

After a minute of trying to rouse him, she surrendered, slipping her doll from his grasp and promising him she would not let the Lurker win. Descending the tree, she gripped her bloodstained doll and sobbed, knowing there was but one thing left to do—repurpose Mama LeFleur's old dolls, so she and the rest of the town might stand a fighting chance.

She ran for the abandoned house, feeling the water rise around her ankles with each step. Amidst the chaos of the night, she clung to Mama LeFleur's words about the storm, finding solace in the promise of a better tomorrow. She had only to make it through tonight. It meant little for Jaxson, but there was a glimmer of hope for the rest of the town. She carried their belongings along in a basket, ready to dress as many dolls as she could.

Perhaps if she saved the townspeople, she would earn her place. She pushed herself harder as the abandoned house came into view, its broken windows giving sight to the shelves of glowing dolls within. It was as though an irresistible force was beckoning her inside the open door.

"Been expecting you," Sheriff Hayes said, his eyes fixed on her as she entered the home. He was clutching the axe she had tossed on the porch the other night and wearing a deranged look. "Come on in now."

Lydia stopped short, dropping her basket to clutch her doll with both hands. "Jaxson's hurt."

The Sheriff tightened his grip on the axe. "What happened?"

Behind Sheriff Hayes, the army of dolls shone brightly, their intensity overpowering the darkness. The power they exuded left her speechless, forcing the Sheriff to repeat himself.

"What happened to my boy?"

Lydia choked on the words, each of which caught in her throat. "Lightning. It struck Mama's tree."

The Sheriff's face trembled as he listened.

"The tree fell," she blurted out. "Jaxson was standing underneath it. I'm sorry. He..."

"This has gone too far." Sheriff Hayes clenched his jaw and uttered the words "forgive me" under his breath as he raised his axe high.

Lydia pushed her eyelids shut, squeezing her doll against her chest as the axe came crashing down. She opened her eyes to a jumbled mess—a large shelf broken in half and a pile of shattered dolls strewn across the floor. The room was filled with bright flashes of light, which fled from the fragmented dolls. Whizzing and howling, the lights bounced off the walls and escaped through the broken windows.

With each swing of his axe, Sheriff Hayes sent pieces of the dolls flying in every direction, his expression grim as he watched the balls of light flee. Lydia tried to stop him, grabbing onto the axe, and biting into his arm, but it was no use. Ignoring the pain, the Sheriff continued his systematic destruction of the dolls, leaving a trail of debris in his wake.

From beyond the walls, a deafening force shook the air. The Lurker, drawn in by their commotion, burst through the dilapidated house, shattering boards, and sending splinters flying. Instead of scattering into a disorganized heap, however, the fragments were swept up in a cyclone-like motion and streamed together before the Lurker's current threw them into the swamp.

With the flick of a grotesque feeler, the Lurker sent Sheriff Hayes soaring across the room, leaving his body trembling from the electric shock it delivered. The snakelike appendages of the Lurker reached out for Lydia next, caressing her face, and leaving a trail of gelatinous goo dripping off her cheek. As she clutched her doll, it glowed with a radiance beyond anything she thought possible, and a heat which seared her flesh.

"Don't look at the Lurker," Sheriff Hayes cried. "It's using your fear."

Lydia's body grew heavy as the doll siphoned her spirit. The truth, which Jaxson had desperately sought to warn her about, revealed itself. Life departed from her extremities, leaving her hands and feet colder than ice as her body withered.

The gelatinous Lurker pulsated, its smoky flesh flickering with bursts of electrical light. Beneath its translucent coil, she glimpsed a mesmerizing pink ball, expanding and contracting, while shooting bursts of electricity throughout the Lurker's body.

Lydia tried to drop her doll, but it was too late. Her hands were frozen, their grip on the doll's body becoming tighter with each second. She was ready to give up when, from behind her position, a deep growl pierced the air. Her eyes shifted to the source of the growling, her aunt's wolf.

The beast was immune to the Lurker's control as it charged past. It leapt into the air with its jaws open wide and aimed at the Lurker. The wolf's teeth tore through the Lurker, rendering its viscous flesh in a cacophony of squelches. Static filled the air. Electric charges shot forth from each hole in the Lurker's flesh.

Freed from her trance, Lydia dropped her doll and hurried to Sheriff Hayes' side. Amidst a chorus of alien shrieks and anguished whimpers, she and the Sheriff joined forces to destroy the remaining dolls. With each shattered doll head, a radiant orb illuminated the room, weakening the Lurker until the wolf overpowered it.

They watched as the wolf continued to dig out and devour chunks of the Lurker's flesh. At last, the Lurker, barely holding on to life, emitted a pulsating glow, flickering like a bomb set to burst. Sheriff Hayes shielded Lydia, forcing her into the corner of the room as a massive blast of electricity shot forth.

The wolf let out a final yelp as it absorbed the bulk of the shock, sacrificing its life to save theirs. When Lydia opened her eyes, the storm was silenced; the house had fallen still, and the Lurker had taken another form.

"You wouldn't hurt me, child." Mama LeFleur beckoned, her weakened body writhing with electric pulses and covered in vile, otherworldly fluid. "You're a good girl."

Sheriff Hayes shook his head in disbelief. "I'll be goddamned."

Lydia walked over to her own doll, feeling a surge of anger and betrayal at having been used by the one person she trusted. She raised her foot, ready to deliver a crushing blow to her doll's head, but the Sheriff intervened.

"The Lurker... Mama, can't use your doll," he said, picking it off the floor. "There's still spirit left inside of you." He handed the doll to Lydia. "There's some spirit trapped in here, too. Hang on to it, and we'll make you whole again."

"Is my Sophie the last doll?" Lydia asked.

Sheriff Hayes looked around the room. "It would seem so," he said, kneeling next to her. "Now, I can't have you getting scared. Until I deal with Mama, your doll can still work its evil, do you understand?"

Lydia nodded.

"Good. Now, where's my boy?"

"Mama's house."

"Go to him," the Sheriff said, standing tall. "I'll meet you there. I can't have you seeing this."

Lydia walked to the front door, and turning back

for a moment, saw Sheriff Hayes standing over Mama LeFleur, his axe poised in the air. The Sheriff stopped, allowing her time to distance herself from the demolished house before continuing. As Lydia moved further away from the scene, an otherworldly shriek filled the air. It was the unmistakable sound of the Lurker crying out in pain. Lydia looked at her doll, understanding at last why she could not bear to be without it. It *was* her. She wondered how the Sheriff planned to unite them, and if anything could truly restore their spirits after all the terror they had endured.

Family First

Lydia

Lydia tucked Jaxson into his covers, making sure he would not roll out of the bed. Given his current state, such a fall could have dire consequences. The tree had nearly taken his life, but Lydia was relieved to find him lucid after she left the abandoned house. She waited by his side for the Sheriff to return, sharing with him the news that they had beaten the Lurker.

Once Sheriff Hayes met them, he broke through the entanglement of branches and lifted Jaxson over his shoulder. To Lydia's surprise, the Sheriff then extended an invitation for her to join them and stay at their cottage for as long as she wanted. It felt surreal. All she ever desired was a loving family to spend time with, a place where laughter filled the air, and the warmth of home embraced her.

Lydia made her way into the living room and sank into the couch. "What's that, Sheriff?"

"Tea." Sheriff Hayes handed her a cup before taking a seat next to her. "Thought you could use something to settle those nerves."

Lydia took a sip of the intoxicating brew. "I needed this," she said as she reflected on her time with Mama LeFleur. "When I was at Mama's house, she told me something strange."

"Oh, what's that now?"

"She said we'd all be whole, and that I would find a new home." Lydia rested the teacup on her lap and sighed. "But we're not whole yet. And why would Mama fight us if she knew she was going to lose?"

With a half-hearted shrug, the Sheriff shifted his gaze to the door, and at that moment, a knock echoed through their home.

Lydia tried to stand but found her legs were frozen. "Sheriff," she murmured, as her teacup fell to the floor. "I can't move."

Panic spread through her body as Sheriff Hayes ignored her pleas and headed for the door. Her eyes shifted to her doll, which emitted its horrible green glow once more. She tried to call out, but her jaw had gone numb, preventing any words from escaping her lips.

Whatever toxic brew the Sheriff served her had dispersed to every inch of her body, leaving only her eyes to wander, and her ears to listen. The Lurker's haunting drone filled her ears, followed by a horrid squishing sound as the Lurker oozed its way into the small cottage. It positioned its damaged body in front of her, dripping goop from its various wounds.

Bits of the Lurker's lumpy flesh retracted, revealing a set of semi-translucent, razor-sharp teeth. It desired her fear, and in her vulnerable state, isolated from the man she now trusted, and trapped within a nightmare, fear was exactly what the Lurker got.

Using Lydia's vulnerability, her doll siphoned the last of her spirit for the Lurker. Her consciousness separated from her body, floating through a ghostlike realm until it was vacuumed into the prison of her doll's head, leaving her body to tumble lifelessly off the couch.

"I'm sorry," Sheriff Hayes said, scooping Lydia's body off the floor. "But there *was* one more doll left." He closed his eyes, offering Lydia's body to the Lurker. "Family comes first, you know, and as a reward for letting the Lurker live, she's agreed to return my other half."

The Lurker extended its feelers, snatching Lydia's body from the Sheriff's hands, and leaving Lydia's spirit to watch in horror as it tore her remains apart. Sheriff Hayes left the room, unwilling to witness the reality of his decision.

Within the Lurker's semi-translucent flesh, Lydia saw torn bits of her corpse being degraded by electrical surges, which the Lurker used to repair its injuries. Her severed hand contracted into a fist and released as nothing but mere bones after the electricity passed through it. Piece by piece, the Lurker continued to dismantle her body until nothing remained.

Sheriff Hayes returned, cradling his sister's doll in his arms. The Lurker shifted, its lumpy surface still glistening in Lydia's blood. Unable to turn away, or so much as blink in her new lifeless body, Lydia watched the Lurker coil a slimy feeler around the doll in Sheriff Hayes' hand, while another feeler wrapped itself around his body.

The pink orb in the Lurker's center mass pulsed, emitting a soft, ethereal glow that connected the Sheriff to his sister's doll. Then, a blaze of light transferred from the doll to the Sheriff, and he smiled with relief, but only for a moment before his face contorted. He fell to the floor, clutching his head, and writhing in agony.

Lydia, observing through the eyes of her doll, cursed the Sheriff for what he had done. The Lurker, sensing her betrayal, turned its attention back to her. It showed no semblance of the concern that it had portrayed as Mama LeFleur, however, as it wrapped its cold feelers around her and dragged her back to the remains of the abandoned house.

It Never Ends

Lydia

I cannot say how much time has passed, only that each moment feels like an eternity. Although I have no way to communicate with him, Jaxson still visits me from time to time, his voice filling the void as he reads stories to me. While my lifeless cage remains unchanged, I notice how his body has grown considerably, and his voice has deepened. The stories he reads to me lack encouragement, however, serving only to further my lexicon, so that I might express my suffering in a more sophisticated manner.

The atrocities that occurred around me were too overwhelming to fully comprehend, especially considering my young age. Given the opportunity to reflect, I understand more than I ever wished to. If I had possessed the knowledge, then that I do now, I would have fled, but the Lurker leaves no room for escape. Its influence misses nothing and comprehends everything.

As Mama LeFleur, the Lurker promised that when the storm passed, we would all be whole, and I would find myself a new home. For whatever value it held, she was telling the truth. She linked Sheriff Hayes with his missing half, and my spirit is wholly contained within my doll, living in a new home.

The abandoned house, now reconstructed by Jaxson, is where I spend my existence. The Sheriff's aunt, having spent her entire life in confinement here, had descended entirely into madness. Once rejoined with the Sheriff, her pain, and solitude weighed heavily on his already damaged mind, triggering a permanent descent into psychosis. As Jaxson has relayed to me countless times, the Sheriff is a mere shell of his former self, who will spend his final years curled up in the corner of his cottage, imprisoned as his sister was...as I am.

The presence of the Lurker looms over us all, each of us serving in our own unique way, for it is a creature which requires a community to exist. One not large or brave enough to overthrow it, and whose members are willing to provide just enough outside sacrifice.

Do people truly go mad if they leave town, and can they be summoned back? I do not know. What I know is that only my aunt, the woman in the woods, has ever been brave enough to fight back. To everyone else, the Lurker is sweet old Mama LeFleur.

I have learned that the Lurker never alters its form. Instead, it manipulates the senses of its observers to manifest as Mama whenever necessary. Living from one generation to the next, secluded from the rest of the world. It continues to haunt me—the knowledge that I shared tea with the creature, ignorant of its true form and the sensation of its oozing appendages. At times, I wonder if the Lurker's influence still lingers in my mind, but it seems there would be no reason for it to spend such energy.

As time continues to pass, I perceive the world around me with a newfound terror, seeing it for what it is. The truths I once held onto, such as good and evil, have dissolved into nothingness. These constructs reconcile us with the cruel nature of the world, all while inflating our own sense of importance. Some may argue that we live in an uncaring world, but the reality is that we live in a world which cares only for itself. The sole universal truth I have found is the inherent selfishness of all living things.

The Lurker comes to siphon my spirit at night before retreating to the watery depths, then rises to stalk the town by day. It always has, and it always will. Not out of malice, but out of necessity for its survival, which hinges on the suffering of others.

Likewise, the Sheriff's betrayal was not rooted in hatred for me, but in his inability to confront the world without his other half. Jaxson, in assuming his father's role, serves the Lurker out of a sense of responsibility towards me and a desire to ease his guilt. He will persist in perpetuating the so-called curse, eventually passing it down to his children. I do not know what will happen when my spirit has been fully drained from this doll, but I anxiously await the day as I slip ever deeper into madness.

Jaxson would never break me and allow my spirit to fly free, but I fantasize about what would happen if he did, and what became of all the spirits the Sheriff and I released into the wild. Occasionally, I deceive myself into harboring the notion that their fates were not entirely unfavorable, whilst I am left to narrate my own descent. But to whom do I narrate, and for what purpose? Well, that is a question only a mad person would be able to address. I am sorry to say that I am no better than the rest of the town, or humanity, selfishly awaiting the Lurkers' next victim, so Jaxson's transgressions may grant me a new companion.

Also by Jonathon T. Cross

Stay up to date with Jonathon's latest updates and releases by following his Amazon Author Page:

About the Author

Jonathon T. Cross is a writer of dark and unsettling fiction, whose stories delve into the mysteries of the universe and the fragility of the human mind. With a degree in psychology, Cross brings a unique perspective to his explorations of fear and madness.

When not crafting nightmares, he can be found in the quiet solitude of the desert, wearing novelty pajama pants. Though his writing tends toward the serious, Cross is known for his playful sense of humor and his ability to find light in the darkest corners.

He invites you on a journey into the pages of the unknown, where the boundaries of fantasy and reality blur and the mysteries of the cosmos await. But heed his warning: once you look too closely, you will never be the same!

www.ingramcontent.com/pod-product-compliance
Lightning Source LLC
LaVergne TN
LVHW041612070526
838199LV00052B/3116